MASTERS
of
VOODOO

The Tale of the Ghost Mother and Child

SENA AGBEKO

DEDICATION

I dedicate this book to the boy in Adina, in the Volta Region of Ghana, who's name I cannot remember because we met and talked only one night. Me, a total stranger, this boy took a liking to me and followed me around all evening intrigued by the fact that I was a city boy transplanted into his village, his world. He proceeded to tell me all these stories about things that had happened in his village, what to do and what not to. Many stories he told me, among them the myth of the ghost mother and child, the inspiration for this book. Rooted deep in the culture of the Ewe people of the Volta region of Ghana, (of which I'm part) this boy was happy to share this myth with me and now, I share it with the rest of the world, with a little twist!

CHAPTER 1

Avaga always mulled over why his parents had given him that
name, more so why he hadn't even tried to change it. Maybe because he had come to be so popular by it, it was nearly impossible
to get people to call him by any other name. His parents died before
he got a chance to know them. The villagers occasionally called him
'the lonely one' or 'Yideka' because of this, but otherwise, everyone's
favorite name for him was Avaga. It was often said that a person with a
bad name was already half-hanged and there were times he felt like it.
Avaga, apart from just sounding vulgar, meant something people would
rather not talk about openly in the village; 'big penis'. His name therefore became a sort of release from the pent-up emotions of not speaking
publicly about anything sexual, as was the custom in the village. It was
a linguistic rule that was taken seriously. Children especially, who were
prohibited from using sexual slang, found his name extremely amusing
when they eventually came to terms with what it meant, and the disre-
spectful, unruly type, always found a reason to come to him, calling his
name and then running off in derision. It was annoying and he never
found it amusing, as did everyone else. Tonight, he was in bed staring
at the thatched ceiling that zoomed above his head. Every evening he
would go through this ritual, knowing sleep would take forever to come.
Tonight, was different though. It was almost dawn and he still hadn't
slept. It would not be long before the entire village came to life. The
garboil that came with the break of day in the village was dumbfound-
ing and made it nearly impossible for anyone to sleep past sunrise. The
women would rise early, most of them with their bare-footed children,

most of whom would have loved to keep on sleeping but were violently woken up to go meet the fishermen with their new catch. The children of Adina, as the village was called, were never forced to sleep at night-time as there were many stories told of the horrors of staying up late. These kinds of stories were commonplace and revolved around everything from fetching charcoal at night time to whistling at night with commensurate punishment, which were all surprisingly perpetuated with a spiritual twist from the realm of the unknown. Avaga knew these had to be stories told to ensure children abided by adult rules without the usual strain that came with parenting. Mothers and Fathers in Adina enjoyed a relative ease in raising their children, as the village was rife with superstition. The belief in it was so strong that children dared not break these rules for fear of debilitating punishment from the 'gods'. When it came to offense and punishment, the gods were known to not know the difference between a child and a fully-grown man. Whistling at night was one such offense he always found interesting. And for some reason, it happened a lot. The story was that it attracted the most evil dwarfs in all the spiritual realm; the Azizans. Everyone in the village knew what the dwarfs were well known for, which was just pure physical torment and brutality. You would not catch sight of where the strokes of rattan cane came from but you were sure to see the deep flesh wounds that the incident always left in its wake. The torment would befall through the night and you would hear the most intense screams of anguish and pain but no one ever dared go near the victim's hut to ascertain the perpetrators. Family members present in such households would usually claim to have heard no sound in all of this and would claim to have slept soundly through the night, while the screams of the victim would keep the entire village awake. Avaga was one of the disbelievers and was certain that the parents of these children were the ones responsible and would just beat up their children through the night for their misbehavior during the day. And the children, for fear of mockery from their friends in the morning, would also remain hushed about what really happened and leave everyone assuming they had really suffered an attack from the Azizans.

The fishermen's harvest in the mornings was heavy and that is when the prices were at their lowest. With the village being so close to the shoreline, the noise of the women haggling and hustling for the fish simply made it impossible to have any peace. It was nearing such a morning and Avaga just couldn't sleep. He had no chores or duties to perform in the morning but he knew he wouldn't be able to sleep once the day started. As his thoughts wandered, so did his eyes across the dark room trying to make out the door. He had decided he needed to take a walk. Maybe that would make him tired enough when he got back, and enable him to just drift off to catch a little sleep before the morning madness that came with living in Adina. As he got out of bed he thought about how unusual it was for him to go out for any reason at this odd time, but here he was, making an exception tonight. Maybe it was because there were always villagers awake in Adina and he could have sworn he heard some other villagers' voices in the distance, which only bolstered his confidence to take a walk. He made his way through his almost bare, unadorned room which was predominantly littered with bowls and plates yet to be washed. The major item in the room was his bed and it was not exactly something that would hold your attention once you saw it; it was ugly, made of hard bamboo and coconut wood strips fastened together tightly by coconut fronds. His only cushion was a thick pile of raffia mats that lay atop this structure. It was not the prettiest of beds but he loved it and as he stepped away from it, he couldn't help but smile at the thought of some pleasant memories that had been made on it. He had no door, just a thick curtain of raffia that completely blocked the entrance and prohibited any view of his room. As he broke this partition and stepped into the darkness, he was met by an unusual chill; the kind you get from utter darkness and silence and not the weather. It was still very dark, as the dawn was still quite a way off, and there were absolutely no stars in the sky tonight even though it was clear. The clear nights usually revealed a plethora of stars and they were notably missing tonight. The first thing that came to his mind was to go back to his room and lay down but he had already resolved to take the walk. The uncommon sight of a cloudless, yet starless night didn't deter him. He moved away from the entrance to his room, briefly pausing to decide where he wanted to go since he hadn't really thought about a route before leaving his room. He decided walking around in circles in his own compound would suffice. His thoughts were never-ending; thoughts of himself, his surroundings, the village and more importantly, his current state: sleepless and alone in the middle of the night, unsure of what to do to ameliorate it. He moved about, stopping occasionally to observe whatever caught his eye. There was not a lot to see in his compound, just sparse and exceedingly tall coconut trees that stood in uneven tallies all over the place. This was a general theme in almost every compound in Adina; an uneven arrangement of coconut trees, and his compound was no exception. The presence of beach sand in Adina was obtrusive. It was everywhere in the village, even the floors of the huts that the villagers occupied. He stood for a while looking at a large amount of it in the middle of his compound and kept wondering why it was there when there was already such an abundance of it. As far back as he could remember, it had always been there and had been sun baked for so long it now had an overtly enured look. For some reason, the night seemed to get darker and even quieter, revealing absolutely nothing beyond the aesthetic coconut fronds that had been crafted into a wall around his compound. For a moment, he was pleased with his decision to stay within the confines of his compound. But that was it; only for a moment. For that was when he saw her! The woman with her baby. It didn't matter what he felt like doing or saying. He was frozen to the spot and his mind quickly raced to his childhood and what he knew of her, as she calmly said in the most melancholic way possible, 'Hovinam'.

He was a boy, just becoming conscious of the world and gradually learning all the rudiments of living in a place like Adina. Unlike most boys his age, he had no parents as he was informed as soon as he could understand that his parents had died when he was just a baby. The circumstances of their deaths were a mystery to him, as it was never revealed. He was raised communally; he didn't belong to anyone and took turns sleeping in different homes every night. Sometimes he would stay in a home for a week or more till he felt his welcome was overstayed and then move on to the next place. No one ever wanted to take full responsibility for him, so he was left floating from one place to the next. Of course, everyone knew his situation but lending more than a helping hand in every home he was in, at any moment, was a requisite for being there. There were numerous days when he would be rudely awoken to go help with the harvest of fish. He eventually got used to this sort of treatment and began to feel that his ability to work was his bargaining power to get into these homes. As young as he was, he had learnt not to become attached to anyone in the village. He just knew that in the back of everyone's mind, he was considered an orphan. He never really belonged. There were rare times that he completely forgot the fact that he was alone in this world; when he played with the other children, which happened rarely in the afternoons and at night when all the children of Adina gathered around Gohoho, the village storyteller to listen to all his stories in wonderment. They would all gather around a fire with Gohoho strategically placed at the head of the circle as he awed them with his incredulous tales. There were a few nights when he would alter the course of his tales and tell some that were blood curling and terrifying. Whichever way it went, Gohoho was trusted with the responsibility of awing the children with his stories, and as they came to know, he had been doing it for generations. No one could really remember when Gohoho was born or who his parents were. He was old – very old. The fires around which he told his stories would cast a chromatic shade on his skin, revealing and even deepening his wrinkles. He didn't look feeble though. The cloth-like wrinkles on his face and limbs were deceptive, as he was strong and sturdy, far from the frailty associated with old age. His stories were riveting because of the way he told them. He put his heart and soul into it and with every word he uttered, he had an accompanying action that accurately conveyed his intent. He brought life to the stories he told. Not only did he tell his stories; he acted them out, animated and full of life. He kept a small garden in his compound where he got his food from, but for the role he played in the village, he never lacked. For the women would bring him assorted smoked fish and any other food they could spare. He was revered. And Avaga liked him. No, he loved him!

He told the story once of a man who stole a neighbor's goat and travelled far into the bushes to prepare it, lest his neighbor smell the aroma of the goat. As it was still daytime and people loitered around the village, he encountered quite a few on his way to the bushes. Many of them he even exchanged greetings with. He then proceeded to the location where the goat was slaughtered and a fire made to burn the fur off the goat. He then gutted the animal, after which he threw the entrails away in a garbled manner to mislead any wanderers in the bush who may chance upon it later and suspect what might have happened there. The aroma of a goat being cooked, whether it was adequately garnished or not was always strong and was very difficult to conceal and as he roasted the remains of the goat over the fire, even he could sense that there were many wild animals lurking beyond the bushes waiting for him to finish his cloak-and-dagger activity so they could feast on the leftovers of what was considered a delicacy even among beasts. There were even recorded cases in the village where goats, considered herbivores, would feast on cooked chevon. That was how appealing goat meat was thought to be. He packed up the now cooked meat, and wrapped it tenfold in plantain leaves to conceal the smell from anyone. He knew once he re-entered the village, there would be dogs and knowing how hungry the dogs in Adina usually got, he didn't want to risk attracting them. But no smell ever got passed the dogs in Adina. It was a good thing for him that they could only wag their tails and not their tongues. It was almost nightfall when he was through and by then, the goat owner was yet to detect the theft. The man arrived at his home, happy with his adventure and even more so from his anticipated feast. His wife, without query, was excited at the prospect of having goat for dinner, as they had for so long feasted on only fish for dinner. This was a special occasion. No one had time to probe, or even remembered to. The goat was more important than life itself at that moment. She set out the akple; smooth balls of corn flour molded into shape with hot water, and the pepper sauce and put away the smoked fish, which, but for the goat, would have been served that evening. For as long as could be remembered, akple was always served for dinner in Adina. The only thing that occasionally differed was the sauce or soup with which it was eaten. Akple was constant, even definite; it never changed as the last meal for the day, at least not in Adina. The couple gathered around the food with their three children who also understood the uncommonness of the meal they were about to have and hence how special it was. It was not long after the first hand had touched the meal that two of the man's friends wandered in. A man accused of stealing a goat should not entertain his guests with goat meat but he had not been accused yet and the smell of goat meat was not easily concealed, so they joined in the banquet, much to the discomfort of the family who would have preferred a more private occasion. It was after the meal was devoured that the troubles started. It was the man's friends who suffered their fate first; falling dead, face first. Quickly, his children followed and then his wife. The man was still alive. At least for now. It was not food poisoning for beyond the fence of the man's compound, a group of young boys who peeked through the fence, drawn by the scent of the goat meat, all dropped dead. Faraway in the bush where the man had prepared his stolen goat, wild animals were dying, including all those that had eaten the entrails that the man had left behind. Even the houseflies that hovered over the meat as it was being eaten fell. The people who had encountered him and exchanged greetings with him as he led the goat into the bush were not spared either. It was the harshest of the harsh. It was 'sevoh' the ultimate curse that could be invoked in the village. As the man began to absorb all that was happening around him, he started to realize his folly but it was too late. In that moment, he would have preferred death to disgrace but he had to endure both. He would be the last to go. As Gohoho explained later to us after telling us this story, sevoh was a curse that was commonly placed on reared animals; animals that could potentially wander into people's compounds or farms and hence be stolen. The way it worked was that once the animal was stolen, the curse would become active and within a short time, all the people who saw, smelt or came into any sort of contact with the animal would die. The only exception was the owner; the initiator of the curse. To them, if you forgave the fox for stealing your chickens, your sheep would be next, so it was a ruthless curse, conjured to prevent theft in the village, and as Gohoho told them this story, the intention was to put in them the fear of stealing. He had done this to many others before and that was why stealing was never a problem in Adina. Doors could be left ajar and valuables left in the open and no one would dare tamper with anything. Gohoho told stories that made the children feel all sorts of emotions; joy, hate, trepidation, love, but his common suite were those that put fear in them. The ones that prevented them from getting involved in any kind of vice, and there was a story for every single one. Avaga remembered he would stay up late, and usually would just run to the beaches at night to get away from the people and think about his life as it was. He was young in frame but mature in mind. He was forced to mature quickly. The villagers would say that he had the soul of a young angel but the mind of an old devil. He was daring and liked to think that he was smart; that when two paths diverged in the bushes, he would not take the one less travelled by or the other, he would create a third; his own. The sight of the sea at night never scared him. He always imagined that something hideous would come out of it at night but even that did not scare him. The peace and quiet of it was worth the risk. Although, something did come out of it one night, or at least Avaga thought it did. It was Gohoho. Avaga was at the beach lying atop one of the numerous boats that hadn't set sail that night and had closed his eyes briefly to absorb the smell of the clear night air, and when he opened them again, there he was; staring straight at him. He was scared and Gohoho knew it, but he just stood there quietly with a deep, intense stare just to pronounce the effect he was having. He wanted to make a statement; a statement that Avaga would understand many years later, standing in his compound late at night when he should not have. A statement he took for granted till the reality of it dawned on him. After making sure Avaga was terrified enough, he walked calmly up to him, sat down next to him on one of the thwarts on the boat, placed his right hand on Avaga's shoulder and began a tale; it was a tale just for him. It was a tale that would change his life in a way he never expected it would. The night-time and near-solitude in which it was told only heightened the emotions it built up in him. With the calmest tone of voice, he began.

"Avaga my son, as you are a child born on the land, you are everyone's child, or at least can be referred to as such. It takes a whole village to raise a child and in your case and this villages', this is very literal. I like the night..."

Gohoho paused and then continued.

"Without the night, we could never know the stars, but you see, not all nights bring out the stars. Some nights are made for torture and horror, and you my son, should never be out here by yourself."

The look on his face, even before he began talking, gave away the fact that that was what the talk would be about. By this time, Avaga had sat up and was listening respectfully, nodding only when he paused. He looked at Avaga sternly in the eye, readjusted himself on his seat and resumed his performance for him, his sole audience on a dark, cold night in front of the never-ending sea.

"Many years ago, even before I was born, there was a woman; a dead woman but she was alive; a spirit. She wasn't a free spirit, for she roamed the nights with her baby; her dead baby who was also alive; a spirit!"

Gohoho kept narrowing his eyes every time he paused, as though he was trying to scare him, but Avaga knew it was just part of his style, his performance.

"No one knows the origin of the curse or why she wasn't a free spirit but to be free, she had to transfer the curse. The only way she could do it, was to find someone awake, in the darkest hour of the night when all creatures of the night were supposed to be snuggling away in preparation for the break of dawn. All she had to do was say the word, 'Hovinam' meaning, take my child. The unfortunate victim would then take her place with the baby and roam the nights for all eternity unless of course they also passed it on. The timing was delicate and had to be precise, or anyone who this revelation came upon would die instantly upon the sight of her. So far, no one knew what had become of her. There have been many days in the past when we have awoken to see dead people, men and women who stayed out too late and even couples who may have sought loving bliss under the cover of darkness, only to meet this fate."

At this point, Avaga just wondered how this came to be known; the curse, when the eyes that saw her never lived to tell the story. Gohoho had paused again and was looking intensely at him. He sensed his doubt and it was as if he read his mind when he uttered his next words.

"No one has lived or survived to report having seen her, but it is said that it was a curse that was laid upon the village after a mother and child were both found dead in the bushes in the morning; murdered. Presumably, the mother had gone out late to answer natures call and had taken her baby along with her; only to come to that fate. The elders of the land could not fathom what could have made someone do this, and dreaded the thought of the evil that lay awake in the wee hours of night. Hence, they decided her spirit would never rest. They hired priests to invoke her spirit, to roam the nights forever, to haunt those who stayed out late under the cover of darkness for whatever reason. It was a dreadful period, as people were confined to their rooms at night and could only listen to the noises of the outside world, never daring to venture out. As the years wore on, occasionally people would be found dead in the mornings; people who had supposedly stayed out late. It was either the woman or someone else, but the priests were always there to confirm the deaths as the work of the woman everyone was so terrified of."

Suddenly, the night did not seem beautiful anymore to Avaga and with every wave that rolled in, he felt it would come with something terrifying. Not even Gohoho's presence made him feel safe. After all, he was only a man, also prone to the dangers of the story he had just told. Avaga told him he wanted to leave immediately, to which Gohoho encouraged him with a satisfied and almost glorified look on his face. He had achieved his objective. Avaga would never again be seen outside in the middle of the night. Gohoho had worked his magic on him. As he left Gohoho sitting there, he wondered why he was also out when he knew this terrifying story. However, Gohoho soon started following Avaga, making his way to his hut, which was further out behind where Avaga was going to spend the night. As Avaga got to the entrance of the compound where he was to spend the night, he stopped and watched as Gohoho seemed to disappear into the cover of darkness as he meandered through the closely placed huts. He could have sworn Gohoho had literally disappeared, but part of him doubted this. Unsettled, he ran indoors telling himself he would never face the night again, at least not alone.

Avaga was still standing in his compound, lost in his childhood thoughts when another utterance of "Hovinam" quickly jolted him back to his current state. She was just as Gohoho had described her in the story he told him as a child on that beach; her feet were grimy as if she had just come back from an age-long barefooted journey. She also had her baby clasped in an arm folded in front of her. Avaga thought the baby looked unusually large, but whatever he thought did not matter at that moment. It was what she did that mattered. She slowly began walking towards him, all the time saying, 'Hovinam, Hovinam' repetitively. She had a grief-stricken look in her eyes that evoked a miscellany of sorrowful thoughts, almost a combination of pleading for mercy and asking for respite. Avaga was stuck to the spot, unable to move, unable to scream when he knew he wanted to. She came within inches of his face, her baby almost touching him. All his senses except his sight had stopped working. Even his vision seemed a bit murky. He anticipated two things, just as Gohoho had told him; either he was going to die that night or he would end up taking her place, roaming the nights with the baby. He just didn't know which, at least not yet.

The morning after Avaga saw Gohoho disappear into the darkness, after hearing that awful story of the woman and her baby that roamed the nights, he was found dead, right in the middle of his compound. He hadn't made it. Avaga was the last person to see him alive – or maybe not. Maybe he had encountered the woman and her baby, or maybe he had died of old age, for he was very old and had passed down many stories and traditions. Whatever the cause, Avaga didn't know, but since the story of the woman was fresh on his mind, he assumed it was that. He kept his thoughts to himself as no one had seen them together the previous night, and hence enquired of what may have transpired. As was the custom, Gohoho's body was to be prayed upon and libation poured before it could be moved. This had to be done quickly before the whole village gathered there. The fetish priest of the village at the time, Vorsah, arrived with an entourage that was smaller than he usually had. It was sudden and he had to make some extemporaneous preparations to get there and did not have time to summon all of his usual cortège. Before he entered the compound, one of his men went before him and poured libation. It was as if the entrance to the compound was blocked spiritually and he had to clear the path for him. It was quite a show, except that there was a lot of sadness with it. A few of the women who had also grown up listening to the many stories Gohoho narrated, muffled their sobbing as they stood and watched from a distance. Gohoho was old and ripe for death else the wailing of these women would have been heard all over the village. The wailing for a person who died young was always different from those who lived their lives fully and accomplished a lot, and it made sense.

"Haaaaaai," the priest shouted out loud at the sight of the dead body. Anybody new to this ceremony would have been alarmed, but as young as Avaga was, he knew it was a part of the ritual. The whole time Vorsah was there, he didn't even touch the body. He just circled it and stopped at the cadaver's head and feet to pour libation. The mixture used for the libation was just water and corn flour. Avaga always wondered why they used that. It must have been the favorite drink of the gods. Vorsah, after a few rotations around the corpse finally concluded that Gohoho's death was not because of the infamous Hovinam but was due to natural causes. That concluded his spiritual autopsy as his men wrapped up the body in large calico cloths and followed Vorsah to the burial grounds where he was to perform the rites to lead him safely to the land of the ancestors. News of death spread quickly in Adina, especially when it came with the break of dawn, and by this time a large crowd had gathered, some crying and some murmuring gossip among themselves. Apart from that, it was no ordinary death, it was Gohoho's death. For some people, it merely meant the end to wonderful nights of incredible folklore narration. To Avaga, it meant a lot more but he could not get any closer than he was to him. He was only a child and children were the last in any procession in such circumstances. He followed anyway, sad but also somewhat pleased that he was the very last person the great Gohoho had talked to before his passing. It was to him that Gohoho had told his very last story; a story that would change his life forever.

Avaga's predicament had not changed. The mother and her baby were still there. It all felt like a dream, unclear and it felt like such a turbid mess in his head.

How could his night suddenly change like this? he wondered to himself.

He had time to figure out what to do but he just didn't know what. He was frozen to the spot. The time that she spent standing directly in front of him felt like an eternity. He didn't think he was going to die anymore, and felt the baby was about to be passed on to him since she was so close to him with the baby almost touching him. He was going to take her place and roam the nights forever. Before he could fully absorb and come to terms with the consequences of what that would mean, he felt himself passing out. Very slowly, his consciousness began to merge with the darkness around him, as the mother blew air into his face. It was unexpected and he inhaled all of what had come out of her mouth. It was swift and everything happened quickly, as he felt his legs give way under him. He drifted off into nothingness. But the last he remembered was her standing over him, with her outstretched arms, with her baby in it, saying one more time, "Hovinam".

CHAPTER 2

"I'm sorry Kuvie, but I cannot allow you to stay here. We will both be killed. Please go away, please!" Kabukor pleaded softly.

The darkness was still very apparent and she did not want to open the door. Kuvie continued to whisper behind it beseechingly, while desperately looking around for any sign of movement to suggest his pursuers were close by. His eyes were fully adjusted to the darkness, as he had been in it the whole night. He could not afford to make any more noise than he already had, as he feared he might awaken others and hence draw attention to himself. He was a killer on the run. Amidst the back and forth imploring and refusal to open the door, Kabukor's heart was racing, fearing for her own life and somehow subconsciously too, for that of Kuvie. She did not understand why he had reappeared and why he did not just scarper off with all the others. She was determined not to open the door, but for how long? After all, he was her brother; the only relative she had left in the whole world.

"Kabu, if you don't open this door, I will be found and killed, please," he continued imploringly, muffling the words under his breath.

Calling her Kabu was her weakness, it was like a term of adoration to her, and hearing it one more time from him weakened her resolve to keep him outside. It evoked memories of good times spent together laughing and pranking others, when he would lovingly call her that. She opened the door slowly and let him pass her as she stood at the entrance peering into the darkness to be certain no one had seen him come in. They hugged each other in silence, tightly, both fully aware that this was temporary and that they would not see much of each other for much longer, unless of course Kabukor eventually decided to go with him.

Earlier that evening, everything was normal. Kuvie had arrived from the farm with huge yams and cocoyam leaves that he had harvested from the farm their parents had left behind for them. But for the general knowledge of the village of their siblinghood, any stranger would assume they were married or lovers. On an evening like this, when Kuvie expected Kabukor to put her exceptional culinary skills to use and make them a delicious dinner, she claimed tiredness. She lay on the lazy chair, sprawled out and seemingly oblivious of the fine produce Kuvie had brought with him from the farm.

"I can't Kuvie, I'm too tired, and I don't want to cook something you wouldn't like. Tiredness impairs our judgment, even with cooking."

Kuvie laughed. He was not the type to get angry with his sister or doubt her words or mood. He had come to understand women through his sister, and he knew when to just accept whatever situation that involved them. He only wondered what she would eat. Even the best cooking pot would not produce food by itself, so it meant he had to cook. The last time he cooked the whole compound smelled like there was a dead rat rotting away somewhere close by. He claimed it was because of the momoni he used, the stinking fish that was supposed to add flavor to the food. Of course, it was a lie and he knew it. After all, Kabukor had cooked many times with it and the house still smelt wonderful. He had to look for an alternative. He didn't want to settle for roasted corn which, in his book, was the simplest thing to prepare. Gathering only a few yams and half of the cocoyam leaves he had brought with him, he made his way out of the compound, assuring Kabukor that he would be back soon. She chuckled at the thought of what he was going to do. She knew he was taking it to his friends, Kadi and Yao. These two were brothers who were very lazy. Strangely enough though, they seemed to know how to cook; at least well enough to always be the cooks when the men agreed to meet and make merry. They were the only two men still known to live with their parents and they were not penitent of it. Kadi was the older of the two and was expected to have started his own household but his inability to do that, many of the villagers believe, had a bad influence on his younger sibling, who also followed suit, never bothering to make the move. Kadi would often say that marriage was like a bag with ninety-nine snakes and one eel, you try to get the eel but you end up only being bitten by snakes. Rumors were rife in the village that their father had also grown up in his parent's household until they both passed, but at least at some point, he married their mother, and they then lived there till he inherited it. According to the rumors, it had become a tradition in the family and Kadi and Yao were not about to break it. The fruit does not fall far from the tree, they say.

Kabukor watched him go, thinking to herself how lucky she was to have a brother who was nothing like the duo, Kadi and Yao. She allowed her mind to wander, thinking about other things, womanly things, and slowly she closed her eyes to catch some rest as her brother's image continued to grow smaller, slowly disappearing.

A few minutes later, Kuvie arrived at his destination. On his way, he had encountered a mob of villagers, mostly women, who were returning from the riverside. They thronged his path, asking him to reserve yams for them, as he had done for some of them during the past yam season. Those who were not previously at the receiving end of his generosity also implored him, saying that it was their turn to claim their yam. Kuvie was benevolent, but knew he would not be able to give as many yams, as the requests he received far outnumbered those he had growing in the soil. Aside from that, he needed to store some away for himself. It was going to be difficult and he knew he would end up in the bad books of some of these women. He looked around the compound, and Yao was the only one in sight. Yao had not noticed the presence of Kuvie, as he seemed engrossed in sharpening a cutlass and he had a few others that lay beside him that were yet to touch the black stone he was grinding them away on. Kuvie crept slowly up to him, intending to surprise him. As he got to him, Kadi appeared from around the corner of the house, holding what looked like an old broken spear in his left hand, and other small, crude and unrecognizable tools in the other hand. Kadi was pleasantly surprised to see Kuvie, and he shouted his name in excitement, effectively ruining the intended surprise on Yao, who turned immediately. They were both always excited to see Kuvie. To them, the sight of Kuvie was synonymous with food, and the foodstuff in his arms today re-affirmed this notion. Kadi set the items he had in his hands next to all the others, and wiped his hands instinctively on his loin cloth, as he put his arms around Kuvie, who was happy to see him but more so because of what he had brought, food. Yao, by this time, had turned back to his activity and exercised some urgency, which was usually missing from any routine that involved the two brothers.

Curious, Kuvie asked, "Why the tools and why are you sharpening them? Are you planning anything? Maybe farming?"

With a confused look on his face, Kadi looked at the pile of crude elements on the floor next to Yao and laughed before blurting out excitedly,

"My brother, these are weapons and not farm tools! Today we are going to go hunting."

"I know that they are not farming tools!" Kuvie replied, slightly embarrassed.

"I only asked because I can never tell what you two are up to, or if you know what to use for what."

He was right. Kadi and Yao were the type to try cut down a baobab tree with a small knife. You could never tell.

The best time to go hunting in the village was always just when the sun was setting, when all the animals began to roam again after avoiding the scorching heat of the afternoon sun. Kuvie understood this more than they did, as he usually stayed past sundown and saw various bush animals come out and creep around his crops. But he was not a hunter. He was a farmer and that's what he did, farm. He was surprised at the sudden decision of the two, and queried further, suspicious of their real intent even though he could not think of any other reason why they would bring out such weaponry.

"So whose idea was it to go hun..?" Kuvie started to ask but he paused and, as an afterthought, added, "Ah! But if you knew you were going to go hunting now, why did you not just sharpen the tools earlier? You would have saved yourself the hassle of having to rush sharpening them."

Yao turned once more to look at Kuvie, and as he did with almost every situation in his life, he laughed and wore a look on his face to suggest that Kuvie should have known why. They were just the indolent type; too disinclined to work. His question was ignored as Kadi had already started gathering the foodstuffs that Kuvie had laid before them.

"We will have to go together and come back quickly so we can cook whatever we catch with the yams," Kadi said, completely forgetting that they had no hunting skills whatsoever and there was a good chance they would return empty handed.

Kadi disappeared into their hut with the foodstuffs, bringing out with him a stool for Kuvie to sit on. Their hut was glaringly in need of a renovation. The thatched roof was leaking, with most of the individual strands of elephant grass falling out of their bundles. The walls looked beaten and the deep holes remained to tell the story of many years of bashing by the rain. Kadi's father had done a good job in his youth to preserve the glory of the household, but he was too old now and his sons, who would not do it on their own accord, were also too old to be forced to attend to it. Kuvie would offer to help, but he had been used as a measure of what an ideal child should be so many times by Kadi's parents that he did not want to exacerbate the situation and risk losing the friendship of these two guys. Yes, they were lazy, but they made exciting friends. Not necessarily good friends, just exciting friends. At this point, Kuvie had long given up on any attempt to tell the two that hunting would be a futile mission and that they would be better off just cooking what he had brought, and avoid the worry of having to go into the bushes. He talked to them with their backs turned to him as, Kadi had joined Yao to finish up the sharpening quickly.

"So where is Mama and Papa," Kuvie queried. They were noticeably missing and if they were home, by now they would have come out to see what was happening. Kadi and Yao were making quite a racket with the grinding of the metal against the stone. Again, they ignored him, focused on their engagement. Kuvie assumed they had not heard him and let it go. He watched the two grind away, thinking to himself how that was probably the most work they had done all day.

They were soon done and they all set out towards the bushes. They each had wooden sticks and a cutlass with them. Kadi however, also had his spear. He had reattached the spearhead to a new wooden shaft and carried it proudly. Kuvie led them off the path in the direction of his farm. He did not need a path to get there. They circumvented other farms they encountered. You could not just walk through people's farms without any consequences, especially when it was approaching night time. There were all sorts of dark magic that coursed through these farms, and as they had come to know over the years, people protected their lands and produce with a tenacity synonymous to owning an empire. Kuvie was not the type to do that though. His farm, though unprotected by the usual charms, was unperturbed by the thievery that sometimes thrived on these farms. They soon got to Kuvie's farm and went past it, for that was where the bushes grew thickest and the animals biggest. They had been quiet the whole time they journeyed and they especially needed to be quiet now that they were here. Yao climbed the only tree that was in sight to try to get a good view of what they were up for. Kuvie was surprised at the effort but did not show it. Yao's aerial viewing did not help much, as he could not see beyond the thickness of the bushes. They would have to cut their way through it and hope they would spot game.

They carved their way through the mass of elephant grass and other overgrown weeds and bushes, while all the time trying to spot the slightest sign of life in the bush. There was no verbal communication. Just visual cues, and so far, except for a kill, everything seemed to be going well. Then Kadi saw a movement in the bush; it was sudden and he reacted to it with a reflex that impressed even Kuvie. He threw his spear with all his might in its direction. A very short distress sound with an accompanying thud suggested he had hit his mark. It certainly sounded like it was a huge animal. This was no rat. It had to be a deer or something bigger. They all ran towards it knowing they had a better chance of finishing it off the sooner they got to it. Cutlass in hand, they parted the bushes only to discover what they had hit; a man. Kadi's spear had thrust a man straight through his belly. The impact of the spear was so severe that his innards hung from where it penetrated him and it seemed certain that he would die. Shocked, they all backed away, still unsure of the reality of what was before them. Suddenly, more men burst through the bushes, clearly friends of the dying man. Neither Kadi nor the brothers recognized any of the men but there were a good number of them and clearly, they were also on a hunting expedition, as they wielded spears and cutlasses. The look in their eyes at first was that of shock, which slowly turned to disgust and then anger. They were fast becoming furious and vengeful. This was not a time to stop and think. It was Kadi who bolted first, dropping all his weapons in the process. Kuvie and Yao were both confused. They were not killers but the men did not know that and emotions were running high. They also ran, each in different directions. Kuvie saw several of the men go in Yao's direction. Maybe because they felt they could grab him. After that, he ran with all his senses, never stopping or looking back to see if he was being pursued. He ran till he could run no more. Unsure of where he was, but certain that he was out of the danger of the aggrieved men, he collapsed on the ground knowing that his life had taken a course that he had no control over. The men surely had to be from his village, and he feared they would have recognized all of them. He could simply go back and say that it was Kadi who threw the spear that killed the man, but until that was proven or Kadi was found, he would be made to pay for it. And he knew that there was no way Kadi was going to return to the village, not after what he did and knowing full well the consequences of his action. Death was always paid with death. The circumstance did not matter, the families of the deceased always demanded death; an eye for an eye.

Back at the village, the men had arrived and news had already spread about the incident in the bush. The Chief of the village, Torgbui Amada, quickly organized a search party. He was a short, stocky man who had ruled since the death of his brother who was king before him. He knew all three men and he was very disappointed to have heard the matter, especially since Kuvie was involved, but he had to perform his function as chief. There were no emotions and bonds here. It was purely administrative. They searched the homes of all three first. Not that they expected to find them there, it was just a formality. Kabukor was distraught to hear the news. Already, she was more ill than fatigued that night and this news just worsened her plight. She cried on end knowing it meant her brother would no longer be a part of her life. She cried even more with the threats they left at her door of what they would do to her if she, in anyway, assisted him. She could not believe seeing him walking away earlier that evening would be the last time she would see him. Or so she thought.

At Kadi and Yao's house, the mood was different. Their father was merely pensive, while their mother just talked and shouted on end about how the gods had cursed her with these boys, but not a tear was shed. She had cried so much over the years for them and their actions that she simply did not know how to do so anymore. The search party left with the same warnings and threats of death if any of them were to be found within their compound. This was difficult for Kadi's parents, and they both showed it in different ways, each non-attendant to the other. As the men walked away, Kadi's mother continued her rant at the gods, blaming them not for the actions of their sons, but for giving them such sons. Their father just walked off to his room, all the time just shaking his head.

The happenings of the evening had culminated in this one moment; Kabukor standing with Kuvie's arms wrapped around her. The tears flowed freely as Kuvie told her what had happened and how he had to wait for the cover of darkness to come see her.

"But why did you run, why?" She asked looking at him with her tear glossed eyes in the darkness. He knew she could not fully understand what had transpired and the tension that existed in the heat of that moment and why he had to run. These were not everyday experiences and neither was it something that you rehearse. It was a once in a lifetime kind of fortuity, and Kuvie was not ready. He could not have been. Kuvie hugged her even tighter; a partial attempt to stifle the sound of her cries, which were becoming slightly louder. As he let go of her and attempted to plant a kiss on her forehead, the door came alive with a barrage of knocks and thuds. Someone had gotten wind of Kuvie's presence. This was about to go from bad to worse. In the next instant, the massive door came crashing down with about seven men hustling through the entrance. Even Kabukor had not noticed but with the first knock that was heard on the door, Kuvie had already made his way to the window opened it and slipped through, closing it firmly behind him. Everything happened quickly and the shattering noise of the door coming down coincided with the bang of the closing window. The men were not to be fooled though. They knew he had been there and could only have escaped through the window. The noise that had been created had awoken all their neighbors, and the noise that they in turn made, woke up others. The whole village was now awake.

One of the men had already opened the window and peered into the darkness, but he could not see much.

The stomping sound of the footsteps of Kuvie, as he took long strides through the bush, were unmistakable, and soon the sound of many others followed, all blinded by the darkness but not hindered by it. Kuvie had a good head start on them and as athletic as he was, there was absolutely no way they could catch up to him. But the chase continued anyway. Koku, the man who led the pack was a guard of the king. He also doubled as the executioner of the royal house, but for a long time he had not exercised that role. Not that he longed to do it, but his commitment was to the chief, the royal house and the principles by which the village was ruled. He knew how the rules worked, and at this point he knew death was inevitable for someone. Either it would be Kuvie himself, or unless Kadi or Yao were caught, it would be his sister. She had erred by being found with a killer in her house, whom she seemed to be harboring. It did not matter whether he was her brother or not. Not anymore. Koku slowly began to realize the chase was not going to succeed and it would only be a matter of time before Kuvie completely disappeared. In one last act of desperation he shouted in a crisp clear voice albeit tired, "If you choose to run away like a dog and you do not come back to defend yourself in three market days, your sister will be made to pay your price."

With that said, he signaled the men to stop the pursuit. Inwardly, they were all glad. They knew they were never going to catch up to Kuvie but they still ran because it was their duty, their job.

Kuvie's heart sank when he heard Koku's utterance, but he kept running, thinking about his predicament. He did not want to think it was an empty threat. A life had been lost and someone had to pay for it. He dreaded the thought of what they could be doing to his sister at that very instant.

Back at the village, the guards who remained had already taken hold of Kabukor and led her off to the wooden shackle that served as a holding ground for grave offenders. It was embarrassing for her, particularly since she had never in her life encountered something like this. She had only seen it happen to other people. Her thoughts were with her brother and she shuddered at the thought of what would happen to him when he was caught. The whole village seemed to have lined up to see her being taken away and she could have sworn that she recognized one of the men who so roughly pushed her; she had provided a meal for him. There were countless times in the past when the aroma of her food would draw people to her compound, and as good natured and benevolent as she was, she never turned anybody away. In the village, no one ever denied anyone food, as long as there was enough to go around.

'This man, is surely one of those many who benefited from my cooking, surely, he must remember me' she whispered to herself.

She secretly hoped that he would somehow save her on that account, but a part of her knew that would not happen.

They arrived at the holding ground, which looked like pens for sheep but this didn't matter. Her troubles were too deep to notice where she was going to spend the night and possibly, the next few days. The odor that lingered in the area was something that could not be ignored. It smelt like a mixture of urine and garlic, and that was what it really was. Urine and garlic bonded, and its efficacy was immortalized by a magic so dark that it was far-famed and drew many challenges all of which failed against it. Ironically before this came into effect, the village had been ruled by black magic; a magic so strong that people could randomly disappear from these cages. Captives would turn into smaller creatures, snakes, mice and even cats just to escape confinement. Then there came a time when the priests of the shrines cast a spell upon the whole camp that rendered all other forms of black magic useless. Even then, that eventually became useless as stronger forms of magic appeared, rendering that of the shrines useless. The result was the decision to use garlic and urine. Each, on their own, was known to subdue even the strongest forms of dark magic, and together, the effect was unwavering. It had worked so far, but it came with a stench that was so strong that it clung to the skin of whoever came within range. The garlic that grew in Keta was so strong that people, who somehow did not care about the scent, would carry it on them if they were in public and still wanted their personal space. It worked well for people who showed up late at public activities and wanted seats. People would instantly vacate their seats. That was how pungent it was. This was Kabukor's home now and luckily, a raffia mat had been provided which she lay on, lost to the sights, sounds and smells of the night. She cried silently, wishing that she had cooked dinner for her brother that evening, despite her tiredness. Regret, like a tail, comes at the end, and she was beginning to blame herself.

CHAPTER 3

Avaga still lay on the ground, oblivious to everything around him. He had been there for a while now and the early-morning dew was beginning to fall, gradually wetting his skin. Slowly, he began to awaken to the world around him, his consciousness settling in. After a moment of trying to decipher why he was waking up in the middle of his compound, the memories came rushing to him. He jumped up almost instantly, looking all around him while feeling himself to be sure he was physically there. He rubbed his eyes, and there was still nothing except the darkness around him. Still somewhat unsure, relief began to set in as he thought he might have dreamt it all, that indeed sleep had come to him while he stood in the compound. His body was covered in sand as he made his way back to his hut, but he did not care. All he wanted to do was get back in his room safely and just try to sleep some more. He looked around one more time to be sure that there was nothing out there, that he had dreamt it all. Just as he did, he heard the shrill cry of a baby pierce the morning dawn. It was strong and crisp and sounded nothing like he had heard from a baby before. It shook his very being, sending sensations of fear throughout his entire frame. He was suddenly rooted to the spot. He would have run into his hut but the cry of the baby had come from within. The relief he had felt earlier vanished, replaced by fear and uncertainty. He backed away from the entrance to his hut, all the while fully aware and wary of the darkness behind him for it was from within that, that all this madness came. He found himself kneeling by the mound of sand in the middle of his compound as he cried, caught in the middle of a darkness that could potentially hold more evil, and his room, which now sheltered a mythic mother and her baby, who had come to life. The happenings of the night did not make sense and he could not fathom why he was not dead or roaming the nights with the baby, if indeed she was Hovinam, the woman Gohoho had spoken to him about when he was only a child. In vain, he covered his ears with his hands, trying to keep out the cries of the baby, but it was just too strong. Eventually the crying stopped, and as it did, Avaga buried his face in the sand. At that moment, he had been shaken so much that the only respite he felt he could get from all the madness was to block his senses. Without the cries of the baby as a constant reminder of his situation, and his sight lost to the mound of sand, he eventually drifted into a sleep that he wished was death, never to awaken from. How he fell asleep under the circumstances was a complete mystery.

It was morning and the searing heat from the sand that Avaga had slept on burned him slightly as he woke up. The sun was up fully and he had to shield his eyes as he waited for them to adjust to all the light around him. Just like at dawn when he first woke from Hovinam's trance, the memories of what had transpired that night came rushing, flooding his thoughts with worry and trepidation. As if to remind him that nothing had changed, the baby cried out loudly with the same shrillness that had so many times left him trembling and doubting his very senses. It was daytime now and with the darkness gone, he could go anywhere he wanted – except for the hut. He had no friends to run to and he knew he would be regarded as crazy if he randomly told people about the incident of the night before.

'Or maybe not,' he thought to himself as he made his way out of his compound. After all, Adina was the land of strange happenings. Things happened there that even dumbfounded the custodians of the shrines. They were supposed to know everything that happened in the land, sometimes even before it happened, but there had been many a time that things had happened that even they could not decrypt. He would have gone to Gohoho, if only he was alive. After all, he was the bearer of that story and only he could have easily answered Avaga's questions, but alas he was dead, dead and buried with all the knowledge of that myth. In Adina, he reckoned, everything was believable, especially to a man like Vorsah, the shrine head who had buried Gohoho and who had been there for as long as Avaga could remember; and that was exactly where he was headed, to narrate his ordeal. Maybe Vorsah would know the solution or Avaga might just tell him the story that Gohoho had told him the night he died, and force him to awaken the dead; the spirit of Gohoho.

Kuvie was famished. Since the previous evening, he had had no food or water since working on his farm. He had instead been involved in two separate hot pursuits, further draining his bodily fluids. The sun was not helping either. It was hot as always and burned with such ferocity; the type that you had to seek respite from no matter the urgency of your travel. But there was no shade or water for Kuvie here. The elephant grass stood tall and spread for miles around. Not a tree was in sight and, save for the heat of the sun, he would have had snakes to contend with as well. He trudged through the bushes slowly, occasionally pausing and raising his hands to his eyes, shading them from the sun to see if he could spot a settlement. He did not have a destination in mind, he just sought shelter and water for the time being. Food was not even on his mind. He was a desperate man. Gradually, his pace slowed and his legs began to give up on him. His resolve to keep going was strong, but he made the mistake of looking back. The view behind was just the same as the view in front; miles and miles of endless elephant grass. He could not possibly still have as far to go as he had already come. He had travelled through the night and his energy was not going to sustain him for much longer. He was a strong man but tiredness will break the will of even the most resolute man. He found himself on all fours, with the grass towering all around him. He was quickly losing his senses to the heat and his thoughts joggled between the incidents of the previous evening and his sister. His sister; he had to stay alive for her. If he did not fight and died out here, he would never be found, and she would be killed regardless. He made one last effort at rising but that was all the energy he had as he rolled over, falling on his back. The sun shone directly onto his face and he did not even have the strength to turn his face away from the blazing heat. He closed his eyes slowly, knowing the end was near. If only he knew that things would change so dramatically since the day before. As he did this, what looked like a big black bird blotted out the sun, with its shadow directly on his face. He briefly reopened his eyes and observed, as prior to that very moment he had not seen any other sign of life. Maybe there was water nearby, but it was too late. He was too weak and on the verge of losing all consciousness. Gradually he faded into nothingness but not before coming to grips with the fact that the bird that hovered above him, was a vulture. A vulture lurking around a dying man always signified the end.

Kabukor had cried herself to sleep and was awoken by the incessant poking of a stick through her holding cell. She quickly got to her feet, and only then did the jabbing stop. She observed about five guards peeking through the narrow spaces of the structure she was in. They seemed content with themselves for waking her up and mumbled something among themselves and laughed. Kabukor could not yet properly decipher any of what was said; she had just been rudely awoken and her senses were still trying to re-establish contact with her being. As she attempted to sit, the stick was pushed through again poking her in the thigh, with the guard screaming at her to get up. She did not understand the words but knew she was not in a position to argue. She just obliged, not even able to make out the face of the guard screaming at her. The door was soon opened and she was instructed to come with them. Still feeling groggy, she followed, struggling to deal with the sunlight that met her as she stepped out. There was an assembly of people that morning, and as she was led away she assumed it was because of her they had gathered; they had come to witness her shame. What she did not know was that it was a regular crowd made up of mostly family members of people being held there for various offenses. Some would try to stay overnight crying to the gods and pleading the innocence of their relatives, and would be sent away by the guards only to religiously return in the morning. For most of them, today was just another day in the continuing process of pleading the innocence of their relatives. For Kabukor, it meant something else; humiliation, the loss of a brother, and possibly the loss of her own life.

She was being led to the chief's palace, a place she had only been to on two previous occasions; once as a child with her parents to witness the coronation of the chief, Togbui Amada, who still ruled, and the second time with Kuvie to present his finest grown yams to the royal house as a token of respect and loyalty. As it was morning, the glare of the sun had fully brought her senses back to life, and she could now smell the pungent stench of urine and garlic on her skin. She had never smelt so bad and held herself together so tightly in a vain attempt to avoid dissipating the smell but nobody cared anyway. It was expected once you had slept within the holding ground.

They arrived to what looked like a council meeting in a long, hollowed room with Torgbui Amada seated at the extreme end of it. His guards, headed by Koku, flanked him, followed by a long line of his elders and queen mothers, and as the line formed to the entrance, the hierarchy of people in the line dropped, making room for ordinary citizens who had come to witness the adjudication of her case. The scent from her clothes was strong and those at the entrance showed their disgust by holding their noses, while others just frowned. She was not allowed to go any further, as her legs were tagged from behind, forcing her to kneel. She was officially in the king's presence. She could not speak directly to the king; this was not allowed. What was worse was that, as an offender on trial, she had to keep her head bowed and keep from looking directly at the king. She was at the lowest ebb in her life; dingy, offensively malodorous and facing a certain death. The King rose to speak, the entire room assuming a deafening silence. As he stood, so did everyone who was seated in the room. The King could not be standing while anyone sat, not here. He spoke with a distinct voice that resonated across the room, carrying with it an authority that could only come from a king's voice.

"I have been told of the death of a member of this village, so gruesomely killed by the brother of the woman who kneels before us and two others who are both on the run. She is not here to plead her innocence. As we all know, she is not the guilty one, but for the crime that her brother committed, she will be made to face the wrath of justice."

He had been briefed earlier about the situation at hand and only needed to pass judgment.

The family of the deceased man was there, looking at Kabukor as the King spoke. Their stare was so intense she could feel it, burning through her scalp.

"As my head guard, Koku, has informed me, her brother ran off but not before he was told that his sister would be made to pay the price of death if he did not return within 3 market days. With that said, let it be known that I have passed my judgment of death upon this woman, should none of the three culprits avail themselves to pay for their transgression within that time."

The King had spoken and it was final. As was custom in the land, the King was perceived never to speak directly to his people but through his linguist, so as he sat down his linguist came forward, repeating every word the King had just said. If anything, it was just for emphasis, and the people greeted the final pronouncement of death with the same mixed exclamations as they had greeted the king's, only this time louder and with more emotion. She was not allowed to speak and at this point in time there was nothing she could say to get herself out of the situation. She had accepted her fate and did not want her brother to return anyway. Either way, it would be a loss, and she would rather die and let her brother live, than the other way around.

She was the last to enter the grounds with the guards and the first to leave with the guards, as they led her back to her enclosure. The crowd that had witnessed her judgment remained undispersed, forced to stay by their insatiable urge to gossip and discuss the possible outcomes of what was turning out to be an epic drama; the killer brother on the run, who had an ultimatum to present himself for justice, or have his sister suffer his fate. At this point, it seemed like the other two who were involved were being fast forgotten and all the blame was being piled up on Kuvie. No one knew he was innocent and even Kabukor now was not so sure anymore. She had always believed her brother and everything he told her, but after hearing it so many times, she was starting to believe it. Repetition usually leads to affirmation and that was exactly what was happening here. The voices were getting in her head. When they arrived at the holding ground, another spectacle was developing; a witch had been apprehended. Witches were a big deal in Keta because they were masters of disguise; family members and friends during the day, and blood suckers and cannibals at night. It is the woman whose child has been eaten by a witch who best knows the evils of witchcraft, and Keta very well represented that woman who had had many children lost to it. This witch was not from Keta though. She had been flying and was brought down by the strong smell of garlic and urine, which rose high in the air. It was clear she had long lost her way because they all usually disappeared by the break of dawn, but this one was still flying while the sun was out and was brought down heavily by the stench and the aura the heat created. While she flew, she did so as a bird and transformed to the middle-aged woman that she was, as she fell. Stark naked, she tried to get up but this combination was the weakness of all things evil, all things impure and ill-intended. She could not get up, but lay helpless and was eventually grabbed by the guards and taken into one of the holding cells. By now the King had already been informed. This happened too often and the automatic sentence without pronouncement from the King was death. They only tried to find out as much as they could from them before they were executed, but these witches were resolute and always carried their dark secrets to the grave. Not one had ever buckled or succumbed. For Kabukor, the focus had now shifted from her, at least for the time being. All she could think about was how dirty and hungry she was, but food was still a long way off. This was not meant to be easy. She was now a prisoner, and they made certain that she felt like one, just like all the others.

CHAPTER 4

Avaga arrived at the shrine out of breath and instantly kneeled and threw his hands forward at the feet of the oracle.

"Help me Vorsah, please help me, I'm dead, the evil that has befallen my house is great and I cannot contain it."

"What is it young man," Vorsah's voice boomed from behind the blood-stained calico sheets that rose so glaringly behind the oracle. "Why do you disturb me so early, what bothers you?"

"It's in my room, Vorsah, the baby is in my room."

"What baby?" Vorsah asked, confused and eager to learn more.

With tears and a great many sobs, Avaga revealed for the first time since that night, the story Gohoho had told him.

"Gohoho told you?" Vorsah exclaimed, after Avaga had told him the entire story and the circumstances that had prevailed that night. Apparently, Gohoho was not the only one in on the story, but this was not a story that he was supposed to tell. This was not one of the childhood stories that were told to keep children indoors at night. This was real and from the reaction of Vorsah, Avaga felt Gohoho had made a mistake by telling him and he showed it.

"And you said she left the baby?"

"I'm not sure but I heard the baby's cry from within and they might both have taken residence in my hut, mother and child."

Vorsah shook his head and jumped instantly to his feet, scaring Avaga in the process. When it came to matters of the spirit world, Vorsah was hardly ever wrong and he felt better remembering only how the previous night, he had sensed the presence of an unusual spirit in the land but could not make out which one it was. He eventually concluded that it must have been old age and that his apparitional senses were declining, only to receive affirmation this morning that he was right after all. He immediately went back behind the blood-stained sheets and retrieved what looked like a belt of cowries, cowhide patches and other items Avaga could not make out. He wore it around his waist as he commanded Avaga to follow him. They were headed to his house. Avaga seemed more confident going back with Vorsah in front of him but fear still lingered deep within him. He knew what he had seen the previous night and even though Vorsah had dealt with spirits all his life, he was only a man.

They arrived at Avaga's compound, with Vorsah performing a few rituals at the edge of it before proceeding. His every move, when it involved spirits, was calculated and tailored to avoid any unforeseen traps or spells. He went through the same ritual at the entrance to Avaga's room before pushing aside the raffia mat that doubled as a curtain and a door. He knew what Avaga had told him was true because the baby's cries were loud and had been ongoing since his arrival at his compound. He was ready for confrontation, as he had come solely to expel this spirit. Avaga followed closely and directly behind Vorsah, not wanting to come face to face with this force. He peeked from behind the shoulder of Vorsah and realized that it was just the baby, placed in the very middle of his bed. He cringed at the thought of it lying where he had always lain and immediately looked around the room for its mother, but clearly the baby had been left behind, the mother, gone. It did not look like a spirit either. It was flesh and blood. Vorsah was confused and chanted unfamiliar words to the baby while sprinkling some libation fluid on it. Nothing happened. It only succeeded in making the baby cry even louder. He approached the baby with great caution, all the while reciting his incantations and throwing fluid on the baby. It was not long before he realized that this was indeed a real baby, a human being. It was clear that the child was male, as he was naked and his genitals were exposed for all to see.

"Are you sure this is the spirit child you saw last night with its mother?" Vorsah asked.

"Yes, yes!" Avaga muttered, still awed by the fact that the baby he had seen as a spirit only the night before was so real before his eyes. He was a big baby and his cries were very loud.

Villagers had now gathered outside, some who knew that Avaga was childless, and even more who knew he did not have a woman, let alone a woman who was pregnant by him. They were all drawn by the baby's cries from his compound. The presence of Vorsah further heightened curiosity, as people who had seen him enter started to gather around. They knew that wherever Vorsah appeared there was always something interesting on offer; either death or the presence of spirits. Avaga had never really had friends and those who stood by and watched, could only peer into the compound through the surrounding coconut fronds to try to catch a glimpse of what was happening. They dared not enter. Their curiosity was satisfied shortly after Avaga and Vorsah came out of the room with the baby clad completely in a dirty old brown cloth. No one saw the baby, but the earlier cries and the way Vorsah carried this bundle suggested it was a baby. They were headed to the shrine. Only minutes earlier, while they were still in the room, Vorsah had made it clear to Avaga that this baby was not supposed to be there, if indeed it came with the female spirit that he claimed he saw. Vorsah insisted, which suggested it was his preference, that Avaga should have been dead, if indeed his story was true.

"Yes, you should have been dead!" Vorsah shouted at Avaga after his initial statement of death had drawn a surprised look on the face of Avaga. "There's only one way we can find out what really happened and how things turned out this way. We will have to ask Gohoho. I will awaken his spirit!"

The walk back to the shrine seemed to be the longest that Avaga had ever undertaken in his life. His thoughts were running wild as he wondered why the ghost woman had picked him, and why the child was left in his abode. Coupled with all the people that stared at them as they travelled along the village path to the shrine, it was turning out to be a day that Avaga would not have imagined in his wildest nightmare. Vorsah had not quite told him if he would be present during the invocation of Gohoho's spirit but since he was so deeply involved in everything, he feared he would. The baby, tightly wrapped and warm, was now quiet, as if to answer Avaga's prayer that it would not cry, as that would have removed all doubt in observers' minds that indeed the wrapping Vorsah had in his arms was indeed a baby. They walked quietly, arriving at the shrine only for Vorsah to inform him that they had to wait till evening to start the invocation procedure. It was a known fact that spirits rarely appeared during the day, whether summoned or out of their own free will, nonetheless Avaga complained to Vorsah almost forgetting not only their age difference, but he was the shrine priest; feared and revered, and to be highly respected. A quick contemptible look from Vorsah settled it, and Avaga quickly became silent. He settled quietly on an old tattered mat, while closing his eyes hoping to fall sleep. Vorsah went about his business, disappearing behind the blood-stained calico cloth that had seen the blood of so many slaughtered animals. But this was not before he walked quietly and undetected up to Avaga, blowing a powder-like substance over his face. It needed just one inhalation and when he next opened his eyes, indeed it was nightfall. He had slept all through the day.

⸺◦⟪◉⟫◦⸺

News of the fallen witch had travelled far and wide. Gossip, as fire thrives on wood, thrives on whispering, and by night-time the holding grounds in Keta was agog with all manner of people from within and beyond the village, who had heard of her capture. On nights like this when a new witch had been captured, the guards extended the stay of people to allow for adequate viewing. Sometimes when the witch was from outside the village, someone would come by who would recognize her, and information would be sent out to her family about her capture. On those rare occasions when someone had been identified, the families never turned up. They could not risk being mistaken for witches, as one witch in a family often meant there were more.

Kabukor was still in her cell, all attention taken away from her by this new phenomenon. She had never really come face to face with a witch, or come to the killing of any that were captured in the past, but here she was, within just a few feet of an actual witch. She had eaten earlier in the afternoon; beans with palm oil and gari, a gritty powder made from cassava. That was her only meal for the day. All prisoners here ate once a day, but not the witches. They were dead from the moment they were caught and no one really saw the need to waste food on them, not that the witches usually cared anyway. Their concerns were greater than food. Everyone there had a concern greater than food because facing certain death is always a more pressing matter, and leaves little room for other considerations.

"Hahahaha. All of you are fools! You have no idea the wrath you have incurred upon yourselves by keeping me here. You think you can kill me? You think I will die? All your dark magic will be laid to waste. You just..."

Before the hitherto quiet witch, who had suddenly found her voice could complete that sentence, she found the same stick that had earlier been used to poke Kabukor coming at her with even greater force. It hit her mouth, bruising the cutis of her lips in the process and forcing out a little blood.

"You'd better shut up immediately before I kill you," shouted Koku, who was there at the time and had thrust the stick. "The only reason you are still alive is because we choose to keep you alive. When we are ready, we will kill you with no hesitation and the only regret we might have may be not giving you a more gruesome death. So shut up and await your fate."

She squinted, with her eyes narrowed as she scoffed and then chuckled at what Koku had just said. She remained quiet afterwards, licking the blood off her lips as if she was just finishing a delicious meal. Kabukor observed from her cell, amazed at the witch's confident outburst, but she was after all a witch, privy to so much not yet seen by ordinary men, and she probably had done worse things than most men could even imagine. While all that went on, the whole place became exceedingly quiet, with the only voices being that of her and Koku. Then suddenly someone gasped, seemingly out of surprise. The quietness that had prevailed prior to that made it so salient that heads immediately turned in that direction. Even the captured witch raised her head to look. Her eyes met those of a man who by then had his hand over his mouth as an expression of shock. The witch immediately realized she had been recognized. That would help her cause. Maybe if the man told them who she really was, they would let her go and not want to have anything to do with her. The man however immediately looked away, suddenly pretending that he had not done anything to draw anyone's attention. He was not from Keta and as the villagers looked at him, they wondered what he might know about her. Some of the guards immediately approached him with an expectant look on their face in anticipation of some information, but he just looked away and quickly began to walk away from where he stood.

"Hey you, stop there!" Koku's voice bellowed from beside the witch's cell where he stood. He had also been drawn by the man's activity and was far too experienced not to know that the man knew something. The other guards inwardly hoped this was not going to be another chase, and it was not. The man just stood rooted to his spot as Koku walked up to him and said "Walk with me."

He and Koku then continued together alone, with Koku leading him away from the crowd. He was a strategist and he knew the man would be less likely to answer any questions that were asked in the full glare of the inquisitive crowd that had gathered around the holding ground.

"So, my brother, I noticed you gasped in some shock at the sight of that witch. Certainly, you must know something about her that you want to tell me."

Koku was a tactician, especially at getting information from the various captives he had had to deal with over the years. He knew this man may not readily divulge the information, so as he finished his sentence, he made sure to rest his hands on his knives which hang loosely by his side; an intimidating tactic, as if he would employ them if he denied or told a lie.

"No sir, I know nothing. I have just never seen a witch up close the way I did today."

"What's your name my man."

"Edo."

"Edo?"

"Yes Edo, Edo Tay. I'm from Abor."

Koku looked at him curiously when he mentioned where he was from because it was such a long way from where he stood in Keta.

"Edo, you're a very long way from home. And you say you came just to see the witch?"

"No sir, I was on my way to see my wife and kids in the neighboring town when I heard of the witch and decided to come look."

Without inquiring much further, Koku convinced himself that Edo knew nothing. It was one of two things; either he was never going to say what he knew or he just did not know anything about the witch. Either way, Koku was not going to waste any more time with him. He thanked Edo and started to walk off towards the holding grounds but Edo did not follow. He started off in the opposite direction, not running but taking brisk steps. Koku turned to look at him, surprised that he no longer wanted to see the witch. He watched Edo disappear into the darkness, all the while wondering if he really did know something he did not want to reveal. It did not matter to him at that point anyway. What he had to worry about was the impending slaughter on his hands; the witch and Kuvie's sister, that is, if Kuvie, Kadi or Yao failed to show up. The thing is, he had never killed a woman who was not a witch and this was going to be difficult as he thought of his own wife and daughter. He had pronounced the punishment on Kabukor himself but it was just a declaration of a law which would have taken its course eventually. He was a man hardened by years at his post, but he still had a heart.

CHAPTER 5

"Bring me my ewo!" she screamed at her subjects, as they scurried off to bring the powder she had just demanded.

Earlier, these subjects had brought in a man, unconscious and on the verge of death. It was Kuvie. He had been spotted through the eyes of the vulture that he had seen prior losing of consciousness. This vulture was their eyes out there, scanning the scope of the area beyond their encampment and making sure no one that was unapproved came close. Kuvie fell in the unapproved category as they did not know him but maybe he could be of use to the group and, for that reason alone, he was brought in. They were known as the Adze's; there were many things they were capable of, but resurrecting the dead was not one of them. They could only bring back a man on the verge of death. His loin cloth was removed, exposing all his body and skin to the air around him. Mamaga, while she waited for the powder she had just demanded, had his head tilted upwards as she poured what looked like blood down his throat. It was the induction blood. Without his consent he was being initiated into the group even before he woke. In this place, she did not need consent to do anything. Mamaga was malefic and rarely did she save anyone, but she was making an exception. Under normal circumstances Kuvie would have been left to die and rot, but they had lost a lot of members over the years and they needed new members. Kuvie was vernal and solid; he was perfect for them. The powder was soon brought and she emptied the contents of the entire container into her palm, chanting while slowly blowing it all over Kuvie's naked body. She was alone with him and that was law, no one was allowed in to see how she inducted anyone. She did it all alone and the words she recited were said under her breath so those that stood outside her tent could not hear a word of it. She soon finished her incantations and moved to cover Kuvie's body with a black cloth. She then slowly peeled it off him from the top of his feet and as she did so, he began to shake as if he was being reinvigorated, which was actually what was happening. As she got to his head, Kuvie came alive, coughing uncontrollably. Mamaga laughed at the sight of this, happy that everything had gone according to plan, and placed her hands on her hips reveling in her power. Kuvie, coming to full consciousness, realized this was not where he was supposed to be. He struggled to remember the happenings of the past day, and it slowly came to him. His fear began to turn into relief and appreciation as he remembered how he lay in the field unable to move. He was still too weak to talk and only just managed to focus his sight on Mamaga who smiled at him before he slipped into a subtle unconsciousness, only this time he felt safe.

⸻ ⟨⟨◉⟩⟩ ⸻

Avaga was surprised at how long and deep he had slept. One minute it was day and he had just decided to rest only for a short while before deciding what to do with the rest of it and the next minute, it was over. He looked suspiciously at Vorsah, who was seated across from him, peering into the darkness and seemingly lost in thought. Avaga was sure the baby was fast asleep beyond the cloth that hung behind the oracle, but he didn't enquire of him from Vorsah. He just wanted to go through with the invocation process for which he was there. He was scared, but he had seen worse the previous night, and if indeed it was Gohoho's spirit, he knew he would be thrilled to see him.

"There's some akple and bobitadi ready for you. You'll have to eat that before we begin the process. I know you may not have eaten since yesterday from when the spirit came upon you, so go in and eat to your fill."

Avaga wanted to say no, that he wasn't hungry, but he was and the thought of those moist and warm corn flour balls with anchovies in pepper sauce made it even harder to refuse. He managed a feeble thank you as he got up and mentally prepared himself to go past the blood-stained fabric that he had so many times seen and wondered what was behind. It was nothing special, he soon discovered. It was just a scattered array of items, most of which he couldn't make out, and in the corner lay the baby sleeping peacefully. He quickly grabbed the meal which had been served on a wooden tray in two separate bowls and made an exit. He sat down and started eating, forgetting to wash his hands. Vorsah observed him quietly, realizing how much he really needed the food. He was glad he had prepared it when he did. Avaga soon finished his meal and it was only then that he realized he hadn't washed his hands prior to eating. He was full now and he was beginning to reason functionally. Vorsah went in and brought him a calabash of water; some of which he washed his hands with and some of which he drank. He had wiped the bowl clean with his fingers, devouring everything, so the bowl hardly needed any rinsing. He packed up the tray and headed back where he had picked up the food. Vorsah followed him this time and once they were inside, he motioned Avaga to follow him. Avaga was initially confused, as Vorsah headed towards a wall that was partially covered by white cloth.

'Are they going to spiritually go through this wall?' he wondered to himself.

Before he could reach a conclusion, Vorsah pushed aside the white cloth that covered part of the wall, revealing an exit. Vorsah turned to motion to Avaga one more time to follow him as he went through the exit. Avaga was surprised yet thrilled at this new adventure. He hurried towards the exit, as the baby slept soundly in the corner.

It wasn't really an exit, as Avaga found out once he was inside. It was an entrance to another room. The entirety of the room except the floors was covered in white cloth and he wondered if possibly there were more of those doors behind these cloths, but the mood didn't warrant questions and Vorsah wasn't exactly talkative at that moment. It was business time. There was an oracle in the room. It was an exact replica of the one outside but this one was significantly bigger. Before it, were calabashes filled with various colored liquids, most of them red, suggesting blood. It was rumored that the oracles demanded blood all the time, human blood, but Avaga knew it was probably just animal blood; the product of sacrificial offerings. Nobody ever went missing in the village anyway to suggest it was human blood that stood in those calabashes. The room was empty except for those things; the oracle and the calabashes and now, the two of them. So far Vorsah hadn't briefed Avaga on what he was supposed to do or not do. So far, everything had been motioned to him. He followed Vorsah's lead as he knelt directly in front of the oracle. Vorsah reached into his cloth and brought out a small sealed gourd. As he opened and drank its content, the scent gave away what it was; palm-wine. He had half emptied the contents of the bottle before he passed it to Avaga, who wasn't a complete novice when it came to these things. He understood that often, when there was to be an encounter with the spirit world, alcohol was always employed. Dignity was one thing that could not be preserved in alcohol, yet the gods favored it greatly. The function of it he never fully knew but he figured it served as the medium. He gobbled it down faster than Vorsah had, frowning at the aftertaste of the over-fermented palm-wine. Vorsah pulled out another item from this cloth. This time, it was a feather-like piece bound by a cord. He put it in between his teeth and clenched it as if it was to remain there, but it was only a demonstration for Avaga. He took it out and gave it to him urging him to use it as he had just seen him do. From all indications, he wasn't expected to talk throughout the whole encounter. Avaga was already beginning to feel woozy from the palm wine; he hadn't had some in a while, so the little he had just drank was having a pronounced effect on him. Vorsah was already chanting by now and Avaga could hardly make out anything at this point. He barely managed to stay on his knees. What looked like the oracle slowly dissipated before him, as its place was taken by a man, Gohoho. Everything happened quickly and when he looked beside him at Vorsah, it appeared he had also taken a spirit-like form. He immediately looked down at himself and saw the same. The atmosphere was intense, especially for him. Gohoho began to speak, even without query.

"Things are different now. The mother is tired and she seeks rest. He, that was chosen to handle the child, was chosen because of his good heart and is trusted to handle things well. It shall be well. Just follow your heart."

He had just referenced Avaga without even looking at him. Avaga had hoped to establish the cordiality that had existed between them before but this was different, this was spiritual business and there was no time for frivolities. Gohoho disappeared after those words. Apparently, there wasn't much to be said and both were left unsatisfied, still not knowing what to do, but this wasn't over yet. Even Vorsah didn't anticipate the sudden appearance of the infamous mother of the child as she spoke, taking them by surprise.

"My child, he shall be called Amega. But he will not stay here. You are to journey to Keta, where the purpose of the journey will be revealed. They will be expecting him. The journey will not be easy, but I will be there every step of the way and I will guide you."

With those last blustery words, she also disappeared, not giving enough answers to all the questions they had. What was it with these spirits and giving short unsatisfied answers? Avaga was quite frustrated but this was becoming more intriguing than he had hoped. They were both still contemplating the words of both spirits and hadn't even looked at each other. Avaga was the first to get up, spitting out the feathery amulet from his mouth as he stood up. He was still a bit woozy from the drink, and the shock of seeing both Gohoho and the woman again hadn't quite knocked it out of his system. He stumbled, requiring Vorsah to get up quickly to help him. Vorsah led him through the door that they had entered, all the while also reflecting on the things he had just heard. The encounter was short, both spirits had combined but Vorsah understood what they all meant, but why the shrine in Keta? He understood that it was famed to be the biggest and most powerful ever known, but he was old and was soon likely to pass and needed someone to take over his shrine in Adina. 'If that was the sole purpose of the child left behind,' he thought to himself, 'then he should be at our shrine, to help our shrine grow from strength to strength and to new acclaim.' But that wasn't the only reason Vorsah thought the child should be at Adina. He had a history with Keta, forged in his youthful days, a history that he didn't want to relive, and embarking on this trip would mean reawakening those days in his mind and possibly risking an encounter with people in his past he'd rather not meet again.

But Vorsah knew better than to disobey or displease the spirits. He was going to help Avaga take the child to the shrine in Keta.

Faraway just outside the bushes of Keta, Edo Tay was making his way through the night completely disregarding the dangers that could potentially befall him at night-time. He walked briskly, listening more than he looked, with his gaze fixed upon the path before him. He had just denied knowledge of the captured witch when in fact he knew all about her. The witch he had just seen didn't know anything about him but he knew her. Her name was Shika. He knew because he was part of the Adze's. They were both part of the Adzes, but there was a difference; Edo Tay was their best kept secret – Mamaga's best kept secret. He wielded no special powers and neither was he bound by any special forces, or else the force of the holding grounds would have trapped him. He was just an ordinary man, sworn by oath to do Mamaga's bidding for the rest of his life. Decades earlier, when he was only a boy, he was found by the Adze's in an almost similar fashion to how Kuvie was found. Brought to her by her subjects, Mamaga led everyone to think the boy had been sacrificed to the gods, but she had kept him. Locked away in her private quarters, she watched him grow, indoctrinating him with the ideals of the Adzes. Mamaga chose not to properly induct him by making him go through the blood ritual. For the role that she wanted him to play, she made sure he knew everything about every single member of the clan. In the years that followed his training, he would move from village to village, pretending to be headed for the next one, finding and feeding information to Mamaga. There were also places Mamaga couldn't go; places like the holding ground in Keta and other such places that just didn't allow witchcraft. Keeping Mamaga informed about what happened in these places was his sole purpose for living. Gratitude is the heart's money, and Mamaga felt wealthy in that regard.

"What!" Mamaga exclaimed when Edo Tay told her the news of the capture. He had travelled through the night through routes familiar only to him.

"Are you s..." Mamaga started to ask but stopped when she realized that she hadn't really seen Shika since the previous day. She moved about frantically thinking to herself what her next plan of action would be. She knew she had to act quickly, or else Shika would be killed. She couldn't go near the holding ground herself. No one who practiced dark magic could ever go there, and Edo Tay was only one man. He couldn't attack and get her out by himself. He was a brave man but not very strong. Edo Tay disappeared into Mamaga's inner quarters as she summoned all her people. They came in knowing there was a very serious matter at hand. After all, she never called them all together if it wasn't serious.

"I have just been informed that Shika has been captured and is being held at the holding grounds in Keta."

There was a sudden exclamation of surprise intertwined with fear. No one from this camp ever wanted to hear of that place and especially not about one of their own being trapped there.

"She needs our help and she needs it quickly."

Everybody just looked at her but nobody spoke or nodded their head to suggest they agreed. Being caught up in a place like the holding ground in Keta surely meant imminent death.

Mamaga looked at everyone, not sure what she wanted to say next. Somehow there was a general feeling that someone would be chosen to go on a rescue mission, so no one really looked at Mamaga at that moment. Everyone had either turned away or looked downwards.

"I know what you're all thinking," Mamaga said, looking intensely over their heads.

"Don't worry, I'm not going to send any of you over there. It will be a suicide mission if I did."

A few faces now looked up at her, agreeing with her reasoning.

"What about the man we brought in today? Maybe he can help," someone in the sitting suggested.

Mamaga thought for a while, but she remembered he had already been inducted. Though he was yet to awaken to the reality of his situation, Kuvie was now an Adze and he possessed powers he didn't even know existed. He was still asleep in one of the rooms, oblivious to anything that was happening around him. Edo Tay was also in one of the other rooms, quiet, undetected but listening to all that was going on. He always waited till the meetings were over before coming out. The meeting continued so he remained there. After a long, quiet period with nobody offering a viable suggestion on how to retrieve Shika, Mamaga sent them all away with the instruction to come back with ideas and the promise of a great reward if anyone thought up anything usable. Everyone in her pack was precious to her and her pack was slowly diminishing. She hated losing anyone within the group but Shika was different. She was her daughter.

CHAPTER 6

I t was the break of dawn, with just enough light to reveal two people making their way through the bushes. They were just on the outskirts of Keta and very close to the holding ground. They meandered through the bush cautiously, careful not to make any noise to attract any guards that were potentially nearby. After all, they knew exactly where they were and what they were close to. They passed the holding ground, oblivious to whom or what was being held in there. That place wasn't their mission, they were headed back to the village itself, to see their parents. It was Kadi and Yao. They had tried to find Kuvie but they knew he had ran off in another direction and hoped he hadn't been captured. The bushes that had hidden them for so long finally spat them out and here they were, coming back to what they had initially ran from. They hadn't heard a word of the recent happenings in the village but they knew enough to know that death was inevitable if they were seized. They remained extremely quiet and used hand gestures only when necessary. Certainly, they knew that their compound would be under watch but they did not care. They wanted nothing more than to be able to explain to someone that the killing was a mistake, and have them plead for mercy on their behalf. This was their home and as lazy as they were, they couldn't imagine surviving out there or living anywhere else. The break of dawn was usually when the guards, wherever they were placed, offered the least resistance to sleep. Having fought through the night to stay awake, they usually succumbed at the break of dawn, and this was no exception. Kadi and Yao didn't know this but it played well to their advantage. They eventually made it to their compound where they saw their father seated outside, close to the entrance to the hut. He was an early riser; always up early, either to meditate or just enjoy the peace that came with early morn. He peered into the darkness, his thoughts lost in an adventure, imagining where his sons would be and what they were going through. He also knew that guards had been assigned to watch his compound, and occasionally he would turn his head in the direction he knew they were. It was during one of these turns that he locked eyes with Kadi, and then Yao. He was shocked but reacted swiftly and calmly. He walked up to them quickly leading them behind the house to a small canopy under which he kept some old tools. It was dark and out of view of the guards.

"What happened?" he asked once he was sure they were all out of sight of anyone.

"Your mother has been crying to herself and praying to the gods. Tell me you didn't kill that man."

"I did," Kadi confessed. "But it was a mistake."

He went on to explain to his father the proceedings of that day. Yao all the while just looked around him, still unsure if they were totally safe or not. Their father just shook his head in disbelief, still very much aware of the consequences that lay in wait for them regardless of how inadvertent the killing was.

"I will let your mother know you were here but you can't stay for long. They have threatened to kill us all if you're found here and you know your mother, she might not be able to control herself at the sight of you and might give you away, so you must leave quietly."

As much as they didn't want to go without seeing their mother, they knew their father was right. She was too unstable and, at a time like this, she wouldn't be able to control her emotions.

"Go to your uncle in Dabala, it's faraway and I don't think anybody will be able to find you there. Your mother and I may never be able to make the journey there but knowing you are both there will comfort us. Explain things to him when you get there and let him know I sent you."

The brothers nodded in agreement and both hugged their father, unaware of the tears that trickled down his face as he turned to leave. He had been composed until now, but seeing his sons again and knowing they couldn't stay evoked a sadness in him that would break the heart of any father.

The brothers waited quietly in the darkness as they watched their father disappear around the corner to the front of the compound. The mood was so tense that they had wholly forgotten to talk about Kuvie. Their father had also completely forgotten to talk about the state that Kuvie's sister was in. His primal instinct at the time was only to look out for his own. He went back to his post, thinking about Kadi and Yao and how they were the only two men left in the family to carry the family name on. No sooner had he established that thought than he heard a scream in the distance. It was a guard alerting others to the presence of the wanted men. Kadi and Yao had been spotted. A pursuit had begun already and everything was happening too fast for the old man to comprehend. He quickly darted inside, opening a window to the back of the house where it appeared all the action had occurred. It was too dark to see anything but he stayed there, looking harder. By this time his wife had joined him, also curious as to what was happening. She asked him a series of questions but his mind was too immersed in what was happening outside of the room to pay any attention. A considerable distance away, Kadi and Yao had parted ways, each running in separate directions but the guards were numerous and had split, following them both. As it had already been established that these two, as well as Kuvie, were guilty as accused, the guards weren't only looking to capture them, killing them on the spot was now an option. The noise of the pursuit was heard deep in the bushes, as they had covered considerable ground, moving deeper and deeper into the tall grass. As Yao and Kadi ran, each in his own direction, two significant things happened. First, Yao slipped, falling to the ground so hard that by the time he recovered from the dizziness caused by the impact, the guards were all over him. He tried to wrestle his way out from underneath them but there were just too many, and too strong. Where they brought the ropes from, he did not know, but they bound his hands and feet and carried him triumphantly, heading back to village. Amidst the chanting and singing from the guards, he tried to plead for mercy but no one paid any attention to him. Not far away, the other group that had pursued Kadi were also returning with what looked like a captive, but he was held differently, not bound and just carried by the arms and legs. Yao immediately knew that Kadi had been captured too, and though he felt devastated by at the turn of events, he didn't feel alone. Misery loves company and together, he felt they stood a better chance of pleading their case or plotting their escape. What he didn't know was that a few moments earlier, just about the time that he tripped and fell, the cold, hard metal head of a spear was thrown, tearing through the back of his brother's neck, crushing his spine, severing his vocal cords and stifling any cries or sounds that could have come from the agony of the death that was to follow. The body that Yao saw carried so casually by the guards was indeed Kadi's but what he didn't realize was that it was completely limp and offered no resistance to the guards. Kadi was dead. Yao just didn't know it yet.

Avaga was just stirring up from his sleep. His encounter with the spirits coupled with the wine he had taken earlier had left him washy, causing him to fall sleep immediately he came out of the inner room at the shrine. Vorsah had slept too at some point but he was awake now. For a man who carried the spiritual load of the entire village, sleep was a privilege he rarely enjoyed. He often said that he who slept much, learnt very little. Besides, he had the responsibility of the child now. Avaga at that point was still too petrified of the child to go near it, let alone touch it, yet it needed to be taken care of. Through the night while Avaga and the child had slept, Vorsah scrutinized the child to fully understand what he was dealing with. The most significant thing he saw, which he was surprised he had missed until that point was a mark on the left side of the child's buttocks. It was the mark of the child of a shrine, specifically the Keta shrine. Though surprised, as he looked at it, it became clear to him why the child had to be taken to that shrine. He tried to look for more, but everything else was normal, or at least looked normal. He narrated what he had noticed to Avaga, also detailing what they would need to make the trip. He was not the type to rush things, but even he now wanted to return the child quickly to its destination. A shrine child not in its place meant there was bound to a catastrophe if not taken care of quickly. He gathered what he could; his amulets, a gourd of water, some extra clothing for the baby and some dried meat.

So far, he had given the baby some goat milk, and it seemed happy with it, so he added some of that to his essentials for the journey. The plan was to go with Avaga to his house to get what he needed and then set off on the journey. Usually, cases like this were reported to the village head first before any action could be taken, but Vorsah was making an exception for this one. After all, he had already spoken to the spirits that mattered, and he knew what to do. He didn't want the situation to be marred by any unnecessary debate and argument, and neither did he think the situation needed any more attention than it already had. Dawn was breaking and the first streaks of sunlight were beginning to hit the flora around them. They had to leave quickly. Not so much to avoid being seen at all, but the darkness made it better for them not to draw so much attention. Vorsah placed the baby in the basket it was to be transported in. The basket was hard and rough but he lined it with soft cloth and feathers. It must have been comfortable because the baby, who had been crying, disturbed by being moved, went quiet as soon as his body touched the lining of the basket. Avaga washed his face speedily as they prepared to leave. He could have waited to do that in his own house but in the heat of all that was happening, he was beginning to think the shrine was his home. After all he had spent the last couple days there. They set off, this time undisturbed by enquiring eyes. The silence of the sleeping baby also aided their cause to remain as quiet and unnoticed as possible. When they arrived at the mess that was Avaga's, he quickly gathered all the clothing he thought he would need, wrapped it up in a large piece of cloth, and picked up his gourd which contained the water he would need. He had no food to carry, but both he and Vorsah knew that they'd have to gather food along the way if they were to make it to Keta without dying of starvation. As for the baby, it was only a matter of time before the goat's milk would curdle, and they knew they would have to have something to trade with other villagers along the way for more fresh milk. With all this unsaid and in both of their minds, they set off into the emerging light of the morning sunshine.

The first rays of the sun had just hit the surface of the earth at the holding grounds, rebirthing the obnoxious smell that had guarded these grounds for so long. In the absence of the searing heat of the sun, the stench had been subdued through the night, but not anymore. Prisoners, who weren't poked by the guards to wake them up, were awoken by the stench, grossly reminding them of where they were. Shika hadn't slept at all through the night, so for her there was no need to be awoken, but there was no denying the smell was particularly pungent to her because of her dark magic. Not many people can sleep with imminent death on their minds, but coupled with the torture of the stench, Shika was living a nightmare. The number of people present at the holding grounds had significantly reduced. There were many days when the early morning brought the largest crowds and, with Shika in captivity, that should have been the case. Witches in captivity were always a fascination for people in Keta and beyond, but today it was the chief's palace that was drawing all the attention. Two men had just been brought in; one apparently dead and the other still alive. The instruction for their capture was that they were to be brought in dead or alive and the two, Kadi and Yao, were brought in dead and alive, respectively. It was only when they had reached the palace did Yao find out about the death of Kadi. He watched as his dead body was thrown to ground showing no sign of movement or life. Prior to that very moment he had never experienced the feelings associated with the passing of a relative or even a close friend. Death is a black horse that lies down at every door. Sooner or later you must ride the horse. Yao started to scream, building to a crescendo, and he wasn't holding back his tears either. This was too painful for him. His words though loud, were inaudible, as his tears streamed down his face. He tried to wriggle his way out of the ropes that bound him, desperately wanting to make contact with his brother's body one last time, but he only succeeded in getting the guards to unleash hefty blows on him while tightening the ropes even more. His actions were interpreted by them as trying to escape, which he was, but only so he could touch his brother one last time. The spear that had pierced his throat had been pulled out and it lay beside him. There was a large gaping hole in his neck where the spear had once occupied. Death was feared by many, but when it came upon others, it was always an attraction. Crowds had begun to throng the area, and with the crowds came Kadi and Yao's parents. They tore through the uneven crowd formation not knowing what to expect. All they had heard was their sons had been captured. Their mother, Adjovi was quicker, more dramatic and was far ahead of their father, Kobla, who had the weight of his bulgy stomach to deal with. That was not on his mind though, as they both rapidly tore through the crowd to see their sons. They were both pent-up balls of emotion, ready to explode. Her eyes first met Yao, who held her gaze in a sorrowful look before directing her sight to the lifeless body of his brother, her son. Her forward surge was suddenly halted, as she stood transfixed to the spot, shocked by what she saw. The guards had already moved to stop her in anticipation of her movement, but she just stood there; aghast and temporarily lost in her senses. An almost similar thing happened with her husband who surprisingly broke down into tears first, then took very slow, melancholic steps towards the body but was stopped before he could get near. Only two nights ago, they were a happy family with no anticipation whatsoever that this was to befall them. After all, they lived such ordinary lives that their only excitement was when other villagers confronted them over how lackadaisical they were, which usually brought up only minor inconsequential confrontation. This was different, and the life of their son had been lost in the process. Kobla, when he was stopped by the guards from approaching his son any further, had become violent and was pushing through with all the force he had. More guards came to support the others who couldn't hold back the man who so badly just wanted to touch the dead body of his son one last time. Under such circumstances, bodies were never released to families. There was an incident, long lost in the annals of the history of Keta but still used as a precedent, where the dead body of an offender was released to the family only for them to use dark magic to resurrect his soul. The magic that thrived in these lands had unlimited power and potential, and the old leaders of Keta had long made the provisions to bring them under control. The guards who had gone to help the others restrain Yao's father had been standing by Yao with a firm grip on him, but now that they were occupied, it left Yao with an opportunity to attempt again what he had tried to do earlier; get out of the ropes and go to his brother. The struggle to restrain his father from coming any further was proving to be quite hectic so it was taking quite a while. The man was old but still strong and he persisted, fueled by an unassailable desire to just hold his son for the last time, The struggle gave Yao enough time to work on getting out of the ropes that bound him, as both guards and crowd were distracted. He managed to get out before anyone in the crowd could alert the guards to what he was doing, and he quickly reached for one of the guard's knives from behind him. These were small knives the guards kept in animal skin pouch straps that went around their waist. This turn of events now gave his father the chance to break through and get to the body of his dead son, as all the guards suddenly turned to Yao. Things were beginning to get out of hand. He stuck out the knife, taking a huge swipe at any anyone who dared come close. By this time, his mother was on all fours, crying and wailing to the gods, as she always did in moments of adversity. Very few took notice of her though. There was just too much happening at that one moment; there was a dead body that was being hugged by the bereaved father, and then there was the other surviving son taking a swipe at the guards with a knife and possibly trying to make an escape. That spectacle didn't last long though, as Yao raised the knife high into the air, let out a blood curling scream and thrust it deep into his own stomach. Everyone, including the guards, momentarily froze. It didn't make sense to them. Yao staggered towards his brother's body to be with him. By now, a deafening silence had fallen upon the crowd as they stared in shock and disbelief, with most of them wide-eyed and with their hands over their mouths. His father, who hitherto sobbed over Kadi's body, looked up only to see his second son staggering towards him with a knife buried deep in his stomach. He could not believe it.

"Noooo... Why?!" he implored, dragging the words amidst the free-flowing tears. He attempted to reach his son and was now fully focused on the only surviving one who, unfortunately, was on the verge of death. In that moment, he felt he had failed as a man, and all he could think of was the shame and ill-fortune he had brought his family. His sons were directly responsible for the predicament they were in, but he didn't think that way. To him, he had failed to bring them up as he should have and what had led to this moment was entirely his fault.

Even the guards were shocked by what was going on and just stood and watched, unsure of their next course of action. While they were contemplating what to do though, Kobla, their father reached for the knife buried deep in the bowel of his son, and thrust it into his own. It all happened too fast for anybody to stop him. The crowd was thrown into a state of further shock, completely appalled by the spectacle that had unraveled right before their eyes that early morning. The guards' attention quickly turned to the mother, Adjovi. She was the only surviving member of the family and she had witnessed it all. She too could not believe what was happening. She was near a state of mental collapse, as she looked at Kobla and then her sons. She attempted to get up from the position she was in while she cried, but she felt her senses giving up on her as she suddenly drifted into a state of unconsciousness. She had witnessed too much, and her body and brain just could not process the emotional torture that came with it. There they were, three bodies, father and sons; dead and all bloodied. Earlier that dawn they had all gathered under the cover of the canopy behind their house. If only they had known this would be their fate only a few hours later – if only...

⸻ ⟪◍⟫ ⸻

"Here, take this; eat," Mamaga instructed as she passed a large bowl of corn porridge to Kuvie. "Eat all of it. You're my son now."

Kuvie was too groggy to fully comprehend all that Mamaga had just said, but he reached out and took what was being offered him. The heat of the bowl and the smell of the porridge simultaneously hit him, jolting him back to full consciousness. Just a few moments earlier, Mamaga had tried to question him about his origin, but he appeared weak and dazed, hence the offer of food. He needed it.

She watched him eat in silence, his slurping and swallowing the porridge the only prevailing sound. He didn't seem to like it very much, but there is no such thing as bad food when you are really hungry. It was apparent he hadn't eaten in a long while.

"So, what is your name?" Mamaga asked him as he hungrily ate the porridge. He mentioned his name while looking up at her like a dog at its owner. The blood that had been given to him while he lay unconscious was meant to do that; make those that consumed it render complete submission to her. She thought about the name and tried to figure out where he was from but in a land where they spoke the same language and had similar culture, it was difficult to tell.

"Kuvie, Kuvie, Kuvie," she said slowly and repetitively as she rubbed her chin. "Where are you from, Kuvie?"

At the mention of Keta, Mamaga rose to her feet, genuinely stunned by his answer. That was exactly where her daughter Shika was being held prisoner. She hated anything that came out of that land and within seconds of this revelation, started to look at Kuvie with a hateful eye.

'What have I done?' she thought to herself. She had introduced a child of Keta into her fold. She left him alone in the room and barged into the room where Edo Tay usually stayed, away from all eyes.

"The boy, he's from Keta!" she exclaimed.

Edo Tay stood wide-eyed for a second and almost rushed out to take one more look at him, but Mamaga stopped him. He had seen Kuvie earlier when he came in to report the capture of Shika, but didn't really pay attention to him, as he was sleeping and there was a seemingly more pertinent issue at hand.

"Did he say how he ended up here?" Edo Tay asked.

"No, but I'll ask him shortly. I don't know what to do with him now. He makes me so angry."

"No," Edo said calmly, his face lighting up. "He shouldn't make you angry. Don't you see the opportunity in this? He owes you his life and would have died out there without you. We will use him to get all the information we need about Keta and where Shika is being held and how to get her out of there."

Mamaga's thick lips curved into a smile. She saw reason with what Edo Tay had just said. Maybe this was the solution to the problem. She wasn't angry anymore, and stepping out, signaled Edo Tay to follow her. Kuvie noticed the happy and hopeful look in her eyes as she returned. He himself, however, was downcast. From the time she had asked him about where he was from, thoughts of what had prevailed leading up to his sister's detention came flooding back to him. Mamaga was about to send a barrage of questions his way when she suddenly noticed the trickle of tears down Kuvie's face. She was baffled, wondering what it was that made him sad to the point of tears. She didn't have to wait for long for the answer as Kuvie started his story, detailing everything that had happened up until he passed out in the open field among the tall elephant grass.

"I am sure she's being held within the holding grounds in Keta because that is where all the prisoners are usually kept, and unless I surrender myself within three market days, she will be killed in my place."

This was a distressing tale, but Mamaga's face lit up even more. She now saw the perfect opportunity in this to get her daughter back. If he had a passionate reason to go back there, sending him back wouldn't be a problem at all. She allowed a long pause, filled with Kuvie's sobs, and then proceeded to talk.

"Listen Kuvie, we can get your sister back for you." she said, and watched as Kuvie's demeanor changed completely with that sentence. He looked at her with renewed vigor. Mamaga was a strategist and that was what had seen her through all the years.

"I need all the information I can about the place. Everything that I need to know, even if you consider it insignificant, I want to know."

Kuvie nodded his head at her in an elated, but also confused manner. He was excited but he didn't know why this woman was helping him so much. So far, she had saved his life, and now she was offering to rescue his sister. At that point, he was more grateful than doubtful, so he allowed his mind to rest. All the while, Edo Tay just stood in the corner and observed, out of the sight of both, but very much immersed in all that was being said.

"You will have to go back there Kuvie," he came out saying.

A look of worry suddenly spread across Kuvie's face, but it quickly dissipated when Edo Tay told him he wasn't going to make the trip alone. What Kuvie didn't know by 'alone' meant that he would be well equipped to go but not accompanied by an actual person or persons. He also hadn't been told that he wouldn't be rescuing only his sister, but a certain Shika who was also being held there. Both Mamaga and Edo Tay understood strategy, and they were being very strategic here, waiting for the right moment to tell him.

CHAPTER 7

The mid-morning sun was intense, threatening to burn up everything its rays touched. Avaga and Vorsah had been in it since the break of dawn and had just decided to rest in an old abandoned hut. It was rare to see one, especially since no huts ever stood in isolation. Huts were usually part of a larger village. The occupant of this one must have been a hermit because there were no other structures around for miles. They had decided to stop primarily because of the child. They could both withstand the heat, as they were accustomed to it, but the child had to be sheltered. There was no door to keep the hut shut, just a small entrance, yet you couldn't see past the doorway. They stopped right at the entrance, peering into the hut, but their eyes returned no results.

"I don't think we should go inside," Avaga said, looking at Vorsah imploringly. He was always scared of the unknown and always liked to play it safe. Vorsah on the other hand, was the village priest; he had seen it all. Without answering, Vorsah proceeded with the baby beyond the threshold of the hut. He was in, and his eyes quickly grew accustomed to the darkness, as he noticed that it contained nothing except a pile of dried coconuts and an unusually large pot that stood in one corner. There was nothing to be afraid of in there and he shouted out to Avaga to join him, but Avaga stayed outside still wary of what could be in there. Vorsah's eye was one for detail and he looked at the ceiling and floors intensely to be sure he wasn't missing anything. Satisfied, he placed the basket that contained the baby down and headed towards the lone pot to see what it held. His expression of indifference was visible in his reflection in the water the pot held. He had hoped it would be something else, but his subconscious had told him it was likely to be water, and he wasn't disappointed. Avaga also noticed the copra and the pot and he immediately suspected that it could be the work of the baby's ghost mother; after all, she did say she was going to help them along the way. The appearance of a lone hut in the middle of the bushes seemed to confirm this. The copra would serve as food, and the water in the pot would replenishment theirs. Vorsah, however, still felt there was something insidious about the place, as he carefully scanned the inside of the hut. He eventually sat down by Avaga who had long made himself comfortable on the floor of the hut.

"We will just have to wait here till the sun goes down a bit. I'm not sure though. I think you should try to sleep. I don't think you had enough rest after last night." Vorsah said, while lying fully on his back.

Avaga showed his agreement by following suit.

"I don't know Vorsah, but this whole trip scares me. We have no idea how the people in Keta will receive us or even the dangers that lie ahead of us."

Vorsah knew he was right and he also knew trips like these didn't come without difficulties.

"We have already begun and we can only do what we have been instructed to do. I am confident the spirits will come to our aid if need be." Vorsah said this confidently but he knew they would have to deal with whatever challenges came their way by themselves, without reliance on or consideration of what the ghost mother had told them. With that said, he finally rested his head on the floor. It wasn't long before he drifted off into a slumber. Avaga looked at him as he slept. Just by what he had experienced within the past day, he began to wonder what life was like for Vorsah who had had to deal with issues of the spirit world all his life. His wonderment did not last long as it was overcome by a strong thirst, an insatiable urge to drink. His attention was drawn to the pot in the corner of the room. He reached for the small calabash that Vorsah had among his possessions and made for it. Uncovering it, he drank to his fill, noting how refreshing it tasted. 'It must be rain water,' he thought to himself. Usually, the best tasting water was always collected rain. As he resumed his former position on the floor, he noticed the air in the room had become chillier and the light that shone into the room wasn't so bright anymore. Maybe the clouds had covered the sun, he thought. He lay back and readjusted the pile of clothes he had used as his pillow. He knew he wouldn't be able to sleep. Throughout his life, he'd never been able to sleep during the day. No matter how much sleep he missed at night, he was never able to make up for it during the day, and it was now an established pattern in his life. His mind was fully alert, as was his senses when he started to sense something was different. It was the air that the wind brought in. It was too chilly for an afternoon so hot. Fear gripped Avaga as he began to shake Vorsah vigorously to wake him up. Vorsah mumbled some inaudible words as he readjusted his body on the floor of the hut. Avaga continued to shake him but that wasn't what really woke him up; it was the change in temperature. He had felt it as well. He looked up at Avaga then looked out through the opening of the hut. Without giving Avaga the chance to talk, he headed out towards the entrance, his attention drawn to something unusual. What he saw shocked him where he stood and his countenance was similar. He looked wide-mouthed at the terrain that lay before him. It looked so different from what it was when they had first arrived. From a vast land of elephant grass growing in every direction, it had become a coconut grove, with coconut trees swaying softly in the courting winds. It was a shocking sight that bewildered even Vorsah. He had never encountered a phenomenon like this. Either the trees had grown there mystically while he slept or the hut in which they slept had been magically transported to another location. With Vorsah up and already standing at the threshold, Avaga felt confident enough to step past him and out the hut. He bent down, feeling the earth and touching the low-growing weeds to verify they were real. Both men noticed the alarm on each other's face, which revealed they were both asking the same questions, 'Where are we? Will we ever find the way to our destination or even back home?'

They were still caught up in their telepathic wonderment when the baby's cries rang through their eardrums, piercing the silence that surrounded them and causing both men to immediately run to attend to it. Avaga was surprised he reacted the way he did in running towards the child, when hitherto, all he had done was run away from the child. The bigger surprise however lay in wait for him in the basket, which had him staggering backwards once he got to it. The child seemed to have grown by at least a year. He looked bigger and had more hair and appeared to have even more teeth in his mouth. Vorsah stood by, also halted in his tracks, but he had seen too many weird things in his life to be utterly shocked by this one. Touching the crying baby now seemed to be the issue. He clearly needed to be attended to, but with what they were seeing, it was highly unlikely. He continued to cry, but Avaga and Vorsah just looked on, astounded by what was before them.

"What happened while I slept Avaga," Vorsah asked suspiciously.

"I don't know," he answered, confused. "You weren't asleep for long and the only thing I did was drink water while you slept. Otherwise nothing happened."

'The water!' Vorsah thought. He remembered how often spirits set traps for humans in the form of what they desired the most. Then it hit him! The water Avaga had drunk while he slept must have caused all this. But he was still confused as he wondered if they had been transported to another place or if somehow, time had progressed swiftly, preserving them in their current state. The baby seemed a year older and that gave credence to his thoughts of possibly being in the future, but what about them, there was no hair growth or any sign of the passing of a year or possibly more. Vorsah wanted to find out if indeed it was the water that had changed their situation. He quickly brought out an empty gourd and filled it with some of the water. He only wanted to use a small amount for his experiment, and didn't want to waste the whole pot. He reached into his pants and out came his penis. He proceeded to pee all over the calabash of water. No sooner had he began than the whole pot began to smoke. Not long after, the pot cracked by itself, spilling its remaining contents on the floor of the hut, all the while still smoking and eventually disappearing into thin air. Avaga had already run out, as this terrified him. After all, he had drunk from that very pot. Vorsah, who was more accustomed to this sort of evil, calmly reached for the baby's basket and his belongings and stepped out. He now had confirmation that the hut was indeed a trap they had fallen prey to. The question of where they were remained. The environment seemed to indicate they were in a different location, but were they in the future? But even now, a new, more probing matter had come up; who was after them and who didn't want to see them make it to Keta? Vorsah thought all these things as he laid the baby and his belongings outside of the hut and set about destroying the whole hut, bit by bit with his bare hands, pulling everything down.

⟫•⟪

With the death of the two brothers and their father, it seemed very unlikely that the chief and people of Keta wanted anyone to pay further for the death of the man in the bush. The tragedy that had befallen this family was unprecedented in Keta, and the sadness it created resonated deep in the hearts of everybody, except the family of the man killed in the bush, who felt avenged. The only surviving member of the family, their mother Adjovi had already given up her sanity at the sight of her dead husband and boys and now roamed about the town, oblivious to her own actions of impropriety. The king, Torgbui, Amada who had long been informed of this development, ordered the immediate release of Kabukor. To him, enough people had suffered for the death of one man. It was rare that prisoners of the holding ground were ever released. They were either held there indefinitely till they died of natural causes or were killed as punishment for their wrongdoings. Kabukor's release was implemented immediately and quietly, without the knowledge of the other prisoners. To those who saw her being led away, it meant she was either being taken away for further probing or to be finally put to death. None of the other prisoners cared anyway. Everyone was more mindful of their own predicament than anyone else's. The bodies of Kadi and Yao and their father were all prepared for burial, but separately. As was the custom in Keta, death by suicide still had to be punished so before the bodies of Yao and his father were put to final rest, they had to be whipped; two hundred strokes of the cane on the bare back of the corpses. It was believed that until the final funeral rites were performed and the bodies finally laid to rest, what was done physically to the bodies would be felt in the spiritual realm. Aside from that, Keta was a place that had witnessed many cases of reincarnation, and so the belief in some form of life after death was commonplace. The evidence often lay in marks left on the bodies of dead persons which were manifest on bodies of newborn babies; testament to the fact that it was those same dead people who were brought to life again. The post-suicide whippings therefore also served as a deterrent to those who would be reincarnated, and a reminder of what had happened in their previous life. The whipping ritual was open to the public but performed within a secluded section of the chief's palace. It had been many years since there had been a suicide in Keta to necessitate the application of the whipping, and so many had either forgotten or did not know that this was publicly accessible. There were even more who did not know of the whipping rule for those who committed. Kadi was killed by the soldiers who had pursued him, and as such, he was exempted and his body prepared separately for burial. Yao and his father however went through the whipping, each two hundred strokes of the cane, leaving gross marks where the cane had decimated their flesh. Their bodies were then wrapped up in ordinary black cloth and placed on planks to be dumped in the graves dug at a different section of the public cemetery in Keta. However, a special coffin was made for Kadi, whose body was carried in it alongside his brothers and fathers in a quiet procession to the cemetery. Kadi was buried first in a separate part of the cemetery with the traditional village priest performing the necessary funeral rites before the coffin was lowered, and then finally covered with the yellow sand that was the soil in Keta. The other two, however, were taken to another part of the cemetery where only their kind, condemned witches and other evildoers, were buried. Not many people followed them to this part of the cemetery. The evil that was thought to linger deterred many from going there. It was a relatively quieter ceremony with fewer people. Their bodies were tied up under the black cloth they were clad in and dumped face-down into their graves.

Kabukor had been led home earlier. The guards followed her closely, making sure she got to her hut safely. Even though there was no clear indication that the family of the deceased man would want to avenge their dead member especially considering the happenings of that morning, the guards were leaving nothing to chance. She seemed dead anyway and walked all the way home like a zombie, seemingly drained of life and without vigor. Her release meant nothing to her, so long as her brother remained at large with a death warrant issued for him. She arrived at what was once the vibrant home she shared with her brother. Memories of times spent there with him flooded her thoughts and plunging her into further misery. She hadn't heard about the demise of Kadi, Yao and their father, and was yet to know the reason for her release, but that didn't matter to her. Nothing made sense except that she set eyes on her brother. For her, she was willing to stay alive as long as she knew her brother was alive, otherwise she would have already taken her life. The guards left her sitting on her bed, the look on her face like that of a lost child. They left one guard within the compound to ensure that she was safe. She noticed that the window that Kuvie had escaped through that evening had been left open. She walked to it, peering long through it and visualizing her brother making his way through the bushes in preservation of his life. Tears trickled down her face as she recollected all the events of that night, her brother's warm embrace, the separation and eventually the escape and pursuit. She knelt to the floor, with her face buried in her palms, and in that instant she could hear Koku's voice shouting out to Kuvie to return within three market days or have her die in his place. Then it hit her! She didn't know why she was released. Maybe Kuvie had returned, or he had been captured. The thought jolted her to her feet as she dashed out the door and headed towards the holding grounds, for she knew that was the only place he would be held if indeed he had come back or had been captured. The guard was caught unaware, as he had not anticipated that she would suddenly spring to life and bolt out of the house in the manner she did. His duty wasn't to restrict her but to protect her and his impulse was to immediately run after her. He embarked on this swiftly and judging from the direction she ran, she was headed for the holding grounds, and to him that could only mean trouble.

CHAPTER 8

Mamaga was born into a family with a long history of witchery and superstition. As a child, she had lived a peaceful life with her parents and other extended relatives; all of whom knew about the family secret and guarded it with their blood. At the time, they lived in the island village of Anya, hundreds of miles from where Mamaga now lived. At a glance, they looked like an ordinary Anya family; hospitable and primarily focused on their fishing endeavors, which was the source of food for most families in their village. Very rarely did anyone farm anything except for corn, which was a staple. Otherwise, what was usually eaten off the land was wild and handpicked or gathered. They spent their days just like everyone else within the village; in merriment and going about their fishing routines. On days when all the families would put their fishing implements to rest and mend their damaged nets, they would do the same but it was at night, in the darkest hours, that things changed. Every night by design, they would attach themselves to the walls in their rooms by their feet, serving as a portal through which their spirits would leave their bodies. The sight was one which was indeed frightening, yet remained unseen by the Anya inhabitants. It was at this time of day that they were doomed to be tormented by the roaming spirits of Mamaga's sorcery laden family. Mamaga was only a child at the time, but witchcraft was passed to her long before she was even a child; while she was still a fetus, developing away quietly within the viscus of her mother's womb. Save for her mother's prowess, she would have been killed during birth, for that was what the curse of the craft did; it only sought to destroy. This evil did not linger only within the blood of Mamaga's family, for within the village itself they had introduced witchcraft to women while they were pregnant, only for them to die upon delivery. Pregnancies that were affected were carefully chosen. It was either they were single mothers or had irresponsible fathers. This put Mamaga's family in the perfect position to adopt these orphaned children. It was a recruitment in some way and a way to keep the secret closely guarded, while also portraying themselves as good people in the eyes of the villagers. It was a well-orchestrated move. As a consequence of this, they had at least five other children who lived with them as an extension of their family. Their evil was deep-rooted within the village and fashioned like a treacherous friend; it smiled in their faces and stabbed them in the back. For years, people would die for no reason at night during their sleep. People developed common sicknesses for which there was no cure. For this reason and for a long time, people would refuse to sleep at night, tormented by the fear that they would not awaken to the morning light. He who had enemies could not afford to sleep, and this was an unseen enemy.

All this changed one night when a stranger came through the village. He was old and looked shriveled up, and clearly he had journeyed from afar, the marks of which were evident on his feet and from the dust gathered on his entire frame. Anya was an island village linked to the mainland only by a very thin stretch of land that was bordered on both sides by an expanse of water so people who came in weren't just passing through, Anya was their destination. He arrived right at the onset of nightfall and the hospitable people of Anya couldn't leave a stranger unattended to. They had to find a place for him to spend the night. Usually, as was the custom in all lands, the chief's palace was the place of respite for strangers or visitors but Anya had a different system. They had no chief or palace and neither were they ruled by a leader. In Anya, everyone was considered a royal and it was believed that it was because of this that they were not to be ruled, but instead lived as equals. They also believed they were brought to the island by their ancestors to live in isolation from the hierarchical influences of other tribes around. The duty to host this old visitor therefore had to fall on one of the inhabitants of the village. In pursuance of their supposed benevolence, Mamaga's family accepted to do this, but little did they know that that decision would be the beginning to their end. The old man introduced himself as Gali and explained how he found himself in Anya. His tale was a long and incredulous one that detailed how he had lost his own nuclear family and was on a journey to be reunited with his extended family. He explained that his stoppage in Anya was not only for respite but also for enquiries to see what connections he had over there. He believed he was of royal lineage, and people with such claims always came to Anya to verify it. He had arrived late and he was not to be bothered until the morning when he was refreshed. He was subsequently led to his chamber, a small detached edifice that formed part of the compound of Mamaga's family home. He quickly retired to bed, clearly worn out by the rigors of traveling on foot for so long. As the night wore on, so did everyone else, retiring to their beds. The entire family of Mamaga slept in one room for a reason; to be able to rise together at the same time every night, with their spirits spreading torment through the village and wreaking havoc; spiritual havoc. It was one of those nights and, as usual, they all had their feet attached to the walls serving as portals through which their spirits left their bodies at night and returned before dawn. It was during this period that the old man woke up, well rested but feeling hungry. He walked towards the main house hoping to find someone awake who could provide him food to quell his hunger. It was an unusual hour and rather late but when hunger gets inside you, nothing else can, and common sense wasn't in him at that moment. The wooden door which guarded the main entrance to the building was slightly open, allowing the man easy entry into what appeared to be a narrow corridor. Along that corridor were four entrances, all presumably leading to inner rooms. He checked the first two, all empty and without any illumination but it was the third room that caught his attention, for in it lay the entire family, their feet attached to the walls and their bodies without their spirits. Gali was initially taken aback by the sight and thought it very strange that they lay in that manner but he was an old man and had seen many strange things in his day. After a while, he assumed that that must be the way people in Anya slept for indeed the people here did so many things differently from the regular communities out there. He proceeded to wake one of the children hoping not to disturb any other family member but his soft nudges did nothing to the boy. He then shook the child vigorously to break his sleep but the boy seemed lifeless. As he did so, the boy's feet slipped off the wall, making a thumping sound in the process. Though inadvertent, the old man thought this would awaken everyone, but nothing changed. Something was wrong, he thought. He proceeded to wake every single one of them, in the process disconnecting their feet from the wall. He did this for every member of the household, his fear increasing dramatically for anyone that he failed to awaken. They really seemed dead, and he was afraid. After a few more rigorous attempts to awaken them, he left the room and headed for the main exit from the compound. He knew from being unable to awaken them that they were all probably dead. What he didn't know was that their spirits had merely left their bodies. He knew nothing of this type of sorcery. What he had also done, which he didn't know, albeit unintentional, was that by removing their feet off the wall he had effectively disconnected the portals through which their spirits could return to their bodies. In effect, they were as good as dead. He hurried through the gates of the compound, heading for the narrow stretch of land which had led him to Anya, in fear of what the village inhabitants would do to him in the morning should they find the dead family. Being their guest for the night, there was absolutely no way he wouldn't be blamed for their deaths. He continued for hours, making fair progress through the night. He could sense the dawn was approaching and it was only a matter of time before the dead family would be found and he discovered missing, and a team sent in pursuit of him. He had to make quick and steady progress. Back in Anya, a certain group of spirits were returning from their nocturnal undertakings, ready to return to their bodies through the portals they had earlier on exited from.

The disappointment was apparent, and they noticed with discontent and helpless gloom how the paths of entry to their bodies were effectively blocked. There was one spirit though who found access. One spirit whose body the old man had missed and therefore not tampered with, for she was just a little girl, tucked away in one corner with a body so small that it was hardly noticeable. It was Mamaga. She also noticed with sadness what the situation was at hand, but there was nothing anyone could do about it. After all they were spirits, only able to make spiritual alterations but not physical movements as they would have been required to repossess their bodies. Therefore, as Mamaga's spirit entered her own body, so did the spirits of all the others, cramming themselves into the frail frame of the child that she was at the time. She now had ten different spirits in her, including those of her parents. She walked out of the room, the child in her wailing at the sight of all the lifeless bodies across the room. Her cries soon drew the attention of early risers in the village. The long, unattended cries of a child that early in the morning usually meant something was wrong, and in a village where people commonly died during their sleep, it was taken very seriously. To the villagers, what was odd about this situation was that it was from a household that housed at least ten inhabitants therefore if something was indeed wrong, someone within the household would have attended to it. After a while, when it became apparent that the situation hadn't changed and wasn't going to, their neighbors started to trickle through the gates to query. The sight of ten lifeless bodies in one room was not what anybody anticipated. Soon, with the news spreading like wildfire across the small village, almost everyone had been to the household. Without a leader and someone to take charge of the situation, it took them a while to connect this tragedy with the arrival of the stranger the previous night and eventually detect his absence. A search party consisting of some volunteer males and a few women was quickly organized and went in search of Gali in the only direction that was the exit to the village. He was never found. The funeral held for the deceased was the most heavyhearted ceremony ever held in the history of Anya, with the inhabitants mourning the deceased family months after their passing. Mamaga was adopted by one of the families in the village and in the years that followed, she showed that family and everyone in the village why that was a mistake. With the death of her family and her adoption, she showed a certain new-found sense of maturity and wit about her which suggested that she was older than she appeared to be. She used this smartness to do nothing but evil, doing only things that brought disrepute to her adopted home. By age fifteen, almost all the household members of her new home had passed on and those who lived failed miserably at whatever endeavor they sought to undertake. Even friends close to her failed to flourish. At some point, it became manifest that she was the reason behind all the misfortune. Those who could remember far back to the demise of her original family stopped blaming Gali, the old man who came to visit, and started pointing accusatory fingers at her since she was the only survivor of the happenings of that night. Within a year after the suspicion and accusations, she was finally thrown out of the village, disgracefully ousted on account of being a witch. Though it was true, there was not a shred of evidence that tied her to it, as she had never actually been caught in the act, but she was ready for the road that lay before her, for she had not one, but ten spirits within her. Being a young woman, she was accepted into villages along the way but eventually ousted in similar fashion to what was done to her in Anya. The evil within her was too strong. She tried to settle down in one of the villages she stayed in and start a family of her own and that was when she conceived her only daughter Shika, but even that was short-lived, as she eventually killed her husband and most of his family members before she was ousted again, this time with her child. Together they eventually moved clear of villages and other settlements and gradually started the Adze clan where she lived till this day pursuing her evil agenda, and still inhabited by the ten spirits of her family, a secret known only to her, and not even her daughter.

Kuvie was still worried, seated quietly in a corner wondering about the fate of his sister. He had no idea how many days had passed from the point when he had passed out in the fields till now. He wanted to be sure he still had a lot left of the three market days he had to return to save his sister. The only person he could ask at that moment was Mamaga, and she had convened another one of her meetings with her subordinates. It was odd that there was another meeting so soon when there had been one held only moments earlier. He didn't know what was being discussed in that meeting but overall, he was beginning to learn more things about the clan. For starters, he now knew what they were called. He also knew about the origin of Edo Tay, that he was Mamaga's secret and that he was found only as a boy under circumstances like his. He was yet to be informed about the predicament they had at hand with Shika, but it wasn't going to be long before all that changed.

"Kuvie, join us for a moment," Mamaga instructed him. She was not the type to ask. She always demanded. She had stuck her head out the entrance of the room in which the meeting was being held, to draw his attention and invite him to it. Once in, she began, addressing the gathering.

"I believe you all know the circumstances under which he was brought here," she said, pointing to Kuvie. She paused for a while to observe the reaction of her audience, then she continued, "He is now a part of us, till the end."

Everyone knew what "till the end" meant, and giggled quietly. Kuvie was taken aback by this pronouncement, but didn't show it. He wanted, at some point, to return to his village and resume his agrarian lifestyle. He just stood quietly, still listening.

"What all of you don't know yet is that Kuvie is from Keta, the very place that Shika dared to go, where she is now being held captive."

All eyes immediately turned to Kuvie again, this time with more concentration, but no one said anything. Everyone trusted that if Mamaga saw reason to still have him among them, then it must be very valid.

"He is therefore going to lead our efforts to get Shika out of that horrific place. The original plan was to provide him with whatever fortification he needed, and send him out there, especially since he knows the ins and outs of that village, but all that changed with this morning's developments."

At this point, everyone began to wonder what the developments were. All were young, around Kuvie's age. Kuvie himself was unsure of these developments, like the others, but remained casual in observation.

"Many years ago, long before you were all conceived, it was revealed to me that a child would be born, unique in every way and destined for power and unexampled greatness." Mamaga then went on to recount to her minions exactly how the story went with Hovinam; her death, her curse, her redemption and the journey to place the child at the helm of affairs at the shrine in Keta. She knew this because she was not one but ten souls and all knowledge from those before her was accessible to her.

"This prophecy, as revealed to me, was to start in Adina and travel northwards towards Keta, in fulfillment of that prophecy. Once the child made the journey and assumed his occupancy of the shrine, he would direct the affairs of the village in such a way that he would authorize wars and raids, and expand the powers of Keta in a manner that would put them in charge of all the Ewelands (for that was what all the villages and lands combined were called). We cannot afford to see the growth and expansion of Keta because we all know what that would mean."

When she said this, heads bowed and shook in fear. Kuvie was still at post but more stunned now at this revelation. His thoughts temporarily drifted to the simple life he had in Keta and how now, suddenly, he was caught up in all these complex machinations.

"Now, when I first heard of this," Mamaga continued, "I put in place a few things to make sure this does not happen. I set traps on various routes along the way from Adina, where everything will begin, to as close to Keta as we could get. Over the years, wandering travelers and drifters have triggered some of these, but today I discovered that the prophecy is in full motion and the boy is well on his way to Keta."

Mamaga stopped at this point and laughed a little, before adding, "Well, the boy was well on his way with his helpers until they fell into my trap, so they are now trapped within my Evve." She was referring to the illusionary state in which she had them trapped.

"The child cannot be harmed, he can only be swayed while he's still young, but even so, there's no time as he is destined to mature fully within 21 days, after which his growth will slow down to that of a normal adult's. We need to have him before then, otherwise all of this will be in jeopardy," she concluded, referring directly to the edifice in which they were stood. Metaphorically, they all knew she referred to their very existence, their survival.

"So where does this put the rescue efforts for Shika," one of the minions in the back casually asked. It was odd that Mamaga smiled after the question was asked, but with reason.

"When I first found out about the capture of Shika, I was devastated because I had no hope of getting her back. Then, we found Kuvie here," she said, pointing to him again, "but even with him, though he knows the ins and outs of Keta, we still had to strategize to find a way to get him into Keta without being affected by the powers at the holding ground, since he is now one of us. But then, it got even better; I found out about the boy and he's now trapped within the Evve. Once we get him here and feed him some fiendish blood, with his powers, we can march into Keta and take it all down, including the holding grounds. And then we can go on to expand our territories and enjoy more open and grand lives."

She completed this with a satisfied grin. Meanwhile, everyone remained quiet and was still trying to soak in the full implication of this new development, some content on the surface and others still uncertain about what was to happen. Kuvie at this point was only wondering about the blood that Mamaga had just mentioned. He knew some had to have been fed to him. Although he didn't feel inclined to do anything evil at that moment, he did feel inclined to obey whatever Mamaga instructed, and that was as good as being purely evil himself because Mamaga did only evil things.

She was about to speak again but then she suddenly stopped, caught in deep thought. Whatever it was she was going to say next, she was thinking very carefully about it. Kuvie was close to her and saw the deception in her eyes when she just went on to tell everyone that the Evve was designed to lead them here, that they wouldn't have to do anything but just wait for the arrival of their visitors. The meeting soon dispersed, with Mamaga heading back into her chambers followed by Kuvie with the minions dispersing variously into the other parts of the building while discussing the content of the just-ended meeting. Once inside, Mamaga called out Edo Tay. It seemed like that was what he had been waiting all along for, for he came out instantly. Mamaga had a worried look on her face, a far cry from the reassuring smile and occasional outburst of laughter that was seen during the meeting. She clearly had something else to say to them, something that varied greatly from what she had just told everybody. She waited till Edo Tay was seated then turned to Kuvie and said, "Everything I said in that room is true, except that the Evve won't lead them directly here. I would have to send someone to get them and lure them here."

At this point Kuvie interrupted her, "But who are the others you keep talking about. You keep saying 'them'."

"I was getting to that," Mamaga calmly said. "He is being escorted by two men, one whom I know absolutely nothing about and the other, I know rather too well. His name is Vorsah, priest of the Shrine in Adina. Now, there's a reason the prophecy started in Adina and why he was chosen to lead the journey to place the boy in Keta."

She moved across the room and found a comfortable seat from which she could look at both Edo Tay and Kuvie without having to turn.

"A very long time ago in Keta, the shrine didn't just have one priest, it had seven priests who were charged with the responsibility of taking care of the town. The evil that lurked and operated at that time was so great that it couldn't be just one priest. During those days, I was only a young girl trying to earn a place within this world, lost somewhere within the Eweland, but far away from the happenings in Keta. But I knew of what happened in Keta at the time because the present evil and the powers of the seven priests in defending Keta were both far famed. It was also during those days that the priests fashioned the spell at the holding grounds, which remains in place to this day; a spell that effectively halted the evil in their midst forcing their flight and dispersion to other places, some into obsoleteness. Now, among those seven priests who fashioned this great spell at the time was a young boy in his teens. He was, in many ways, like the boy I hope to lead up here to help me conquer Keta but not quite. Nonetheless, to become one of the seven priests of Keta was not an easy feat and rumors had it that he was the most influential in producing the spell. Over the next couple of years after the spell was made, however, the shrine experienced a tragic period where one after the other, the priests began to die. Every one of them died except the teenage priest. It all happened so quickly that they couldn't find replacements for them in time so, eventually, the young boy rose to become the only priest of the great Keta shrine. This period later became marked by bitter suspicion and discontent at, what everybody thought, was a young inexperienced man at the helm of affairs of the shrine, and who they also suspected of being at the forefront of the death of the other priests; especially since he was the lone survivor. In time, his inexperience, coupled with the disassociation of youthfulness from the position of priesthood, gave his detractors leverage to agitate for his deposition. When he was finally removed as priest, he was also expelled from the village that he had worked so hard to save from the menacing evil at the time. For many months, he braved harsh weather conditions, as well as evil forces that had gotten wind of his deposition. He survived the trip, eventually making his way southward toward Adina where he finally settled. Now this young boy that I speak of, as you may well have guessed by now, is Vorsah, who eventually became shrine head in Adina and has lived there ever since. Now he had embarked on this trip with this boy back to Keta. It wouldn't be a problem if he wasn't involved but he can sense evil from miles away and the only person I can ever really send for this job is Edo Tay."

Over the years, Edo Tay had come to live with the reality of relying on his wits in many situations to survive. He had no powers and the situations in which he was thrown were usually the most dangerous, situations that he couldn't possibly escape from were he to be exposed as a member of the Adzes.

"I'll go and lure them here Mamaga, you know I will," Edo Tay said confidently. He never said her name unless he meant to drum home something he really intended for her to note, in this case the promise of the successful completion of his assigned task. He understood fully what was involved, and he also knew he couldn't accept help from anyone in the fold, not even Kuvie because he had been 'contaminated'.

"I will go in and prepare to set off as soon as I can; enough time has been wasted already," Edo Tay added. Mamaga was impressed with his dedication to her, a clear indication of his gratitude to her. Kuvie looked on, his thoughts still clouded with memories of his sister and desires of home, but very much still aware of the dangers that abound there, especially now that he was an Adze.

As Edo Tay went in to prepare, Mamaga followed, her intention being to brief him on the details on how exactly to execute the task. Kuvie was beginning to grow anxious; eager to go back to try to rescue his sister. If only he knew his friends, Kadi and Yao were long dead and buried, and that his sister was already a free woman. He was planning something drastic. Meanwhile, Mamaga had planned Edo Tay's mission completely around Vorsah and how to lure him into their fold. What she had completely forgotten or maybe didn't know was that Avaga wasn't just on the trip for no reason. The prophesy was bigger than her, and every person involved had a significant role to play in getting the child to his rightful place within Keta. After all, the shrine had been priest-less since the departure of Vorsah those many years ago, and the child was indeed intended to change that. The role that Avaga had to play, which they all currently knew nothing about, was something Edo Tay would have to find out on his own; an encounter that would change his life and direction forever.

CHAPTER 9

She sped on, pushing aside all foliage in her way. The guard who ran after her couldn't believe the deftness with which Kabukor ran. Clearly, she was fueled by a passion of some sort. She lost the guard in no time, leaving behind only dust for him to track. One would have thought that, with the way she ran, she would barge into the holding grounds and start to look through the cages, but she was smarter than that. She knew the whole area was guarded, and barging in like that would not be taken too kindly by the guards who were all over the place. She found an elevated area that provided a view over the holding grounds and spied the cages as hard as she could from behind a pile of abandoned firewood. She noticed no changes in the cages except for hers which was still empty. With no sight of her brother, her thoughts wandered back to why she had been released. She still hadn't heard of the death of the brothers and their father. Just as she was about to turn to leave, she heard the rustle of leaves behind her. It was a person, and it was either the guard who had pursued her earlier on or, the one from the holding grounds. She didn't choose the latter. She waited till the person came into view; the sight of which shocked her. It was Kadi and Yao's mother, Adjovi. It was quite a shock to Kabukor, as she was still oblivious to the happenings of the morning. Adjovi was partially naked, and even the cloth that covered parts of her were torn. She was beginning to emit a pungent smell, which was the first thing Kabukor sensed even before the sight of her.

"Ma," Kabukor whispered, too embarrassed to even hold her nose, "what happened to you, why are you like this?"

She momentarily forgot about her problems, and it was beginning to dawn on her that Adjovi might be mentally distressed. Adjovi didn't respond to her question and continued to move, appearing to be transfixed. Her entire frame moved in an errant fashion, but she somehow remained calm. She had a sad look on her face and seemed to be on the verge of tears but never quite going past that point. It was like an eternal expression drawn on her face.

"Come here, I'll take you to your family," Kabukor said, and reached for her arm. As she did so, there was a sudden change in Adjovi's demeanor. She pulled her arm back, almost snarling like a dog. Her face, which had hitherto just held a sad expression, came alive with tears and she found her voice, saying a lot of things but the words, muffled by her sobbing, made no sense. The guards were immediately drawn to the noise. Sensing the presence of possible intruders, they moved hurriedly towards the noise. Kabukor knew her discovery there would raise suspicion and enquiry into why she was spying on the holding ground, for that was the only reason why she would be in that area. She didn't have time to think, and as she struggled to figure something out, Adjovi broke into a run, heading towards the holding grounds and crashing into the guards in the process. Her hysterical behavior, coupled with the guards' knowledge of the happenings of that morning, dulled the urge of the guards to probe further, stopping to restrain her. She couldn't be consoled; her trigger point had been touched and her recently-acquired fey qualities were in full display. Meanwhile, Kabukor waited behind the stack of old firewood, relieved that Adjovi had obstructed her discovery but still baffled as to her weird state or the reasons for it. A few of the guards finally managed to restrain her and dragged her away, unsure of where to take her. After all, her family was gone and she couldn't take care of herself considering the state she was in. As they led her away, some of the guards remained briefly, discussing among themselves the happenings of that morning. Kabukor listened in, wide-eyed and open-mouthed, shocked at the turn of events. She began to understand the reason behind Adjovi's mental condition. She began to feel guilty that all that blood had to be spilt for her to be released and she started to even feel directly responsible for Adjovi's mental state.

The rest of the guards moved away but she was too shocked to run off. She remained in her crouched position, analyzing everything she had just heard. What struck her the most was that her brother could potentially return without much inquisition or worry about being prosecuted, because she now knew that he wasn't responsible for the death of the man in the bush. She eventually raised her head just in time to see Adjovi been taken off in the direction of the chief's palace. Clearly, the guards needed some direction on what to do with her. She waited a while longer, observing the movements around the holding grounds. She could hardly remember what being in that cage felt like. Her mind was too clouded at the time to fully observe her physical surroundings, but she remembered Shika and the drama she had brought with her. As usual, there was a small gathering of people who had come to observe her. News of her capture had travelled far and those who could, made sure to make the trip.

With nothing more to observe, Kabukor turned back for home, thinking of possible ways to try to reach her brother. It was going to be difficult; she didn't even know his whereabouts. She had barely taken ten steps when her attention was drawn to a sudden outburst of noise from the holding grounds. She tiptoed back, observing as the guards cleared everyone out in the area. Everyone was being instructed to leave and this was highly unusual. She noted with rapt attention how they made sure to lead everyone away from the area, the intention being to clear them a great distance away from the holding grounds where they would no longer be able to observe anything. It was only late in the afternoon and people were more used to being driven out at night time, but there was no reluctance to leave on the part of anyone. Kabukor stayed in her position carefully hidden behind the old firewood, her curiosity heightened more now than ever. The whole area was now clear of people except for the guards and prisoners, but nothing else happened. It was another half hour before there was any sort of activity, with some guards bringing in, what looked like, a portable cage covered with a thick black cloth. Shika's cage was immediately opened and the contents of a small container were forcibly fed to her. Her movements began to slow down as she tardily succumbed to the influence of the contents of the container. Out cold, she was hurriedly placed in the portable cage and covered with the black cloth. The other prisoners just observed, unsure of what she was being taken away for, especially under such unusual circumstances. Kabukor, at that point, decided she was going to find out where Shika was being taken, and what for. As the guards moved with their load, so did she. She didn't know the bushes too well but she relied on common sense, hiding behind anything large enough to conceal her, as she moved along the top ridges around the holding ground area. She continued along the high path she was on, stopping only to see if anyone was onto her. It was hard to move quietly when there were so many dry leaves and twigs along the way. She finally reached a spot where she had an open view of them leading right up to what appeared to be a hidden entry point to the Chiefs palace behind it. She didn't understand what the urgency was when they could have just waited till night time. She noticed that right at the entrance, the guards passed the covered cage to another group of guards situated inside the palace, who then passed on a similarly covered item to them. It was an exchange of some sort, but whatever it was, it was clearly intended to deceive anyone who might have seen them carry Shika away. The entrance was immediately locked as the guards, who now had a different but indistinguishable consignment, headed back in the direction from which they came. Kabukor waited a while to make sure there weren't any further surprises from the guards who had just locked themselves in the palace before she retraced her steps along the high ridges that provided her with an aerial view of all that was unfolding. The journey back to the holding grounds was the same, filled with extreme caution and occasional disappearances behind trees to avoid being seen. She eventually ended up where she had started from; behind the pile of old, decomposing firewood. The sun was beginning to set and visibility around the holding ground was poor, but everything within sight was still perceptible. The guards soon uncovered the cage revealing Shika in the cage, or so it appeared. Whoever it was had similar clothes on; a long black dress with folderals at the end of it, and thick multi-colored beads on both hands and feet. She was still unconscious and, apart from the guards, only Kabukor knew that whoever it was, was also under the influence of what had been fed to Shika earlier before she was taken away. Kabukor watched as she was tossed into one of the main cages like a log. They then picked up the cage she had been transported in and left. Whoever it was bore a striking resemblance to Shika but it was clear to Kabukor that the bodies had been swapped and it wasn't Shika in the cage.

"There she is!" a voice shouted from behind Kabukor. The guard who had initially ran after her when she left home had caught up with her, apparently after getting many more to help him. It was evident by their faces that they knew she had seen what had transpired in its entirety, and immediately went after her. Kabukor, who was startled from the moment she heard the voice behind her, had already taken up quite a lead but headed in the wrong direction, or maybe the only direction; the holding grounds. She moved with the same deftness that she earlier exhibited when she ran from home, but this time it was different; there were guards all over and those in pursuit were a lot more swift and agile than the one guard she had had to contend with earlier. She ran through the actual grounds, meandering between the cages and agitating the inmates in the process. The entire place was agog with all manner of noises from the inmates and orders being shouted by the guards. As Kabukor passed the cage that held Shika, she noticed with surprise the still-inanimate figure of the body that lay inside, and in that temporary moment of distraction, she crashed head first into a firmly rooted pole designated for whipping to death incorrigible inmates. It had been a while since it had been used, but it had just served them well. Severely contused and dizzy, the guards quickly swarmed over her. Orders were immediately sent out to bring back the prisoner transport cage. She wasn't going to be kept within the holding grounds; she was going to be taken away. As vertiginous as she was, her mind was still working, more stunned from who she had recognized in that prison cage than the impact from the head-on collision with the pole. The transformation was near perfect but she had seen Shika at close range while she was held there, and had just seen Adjovi, she knew that was her. Kabukor's sighting and knowledge of the whole exchange made it easier for her to detect the flaws in the disguise of Adjovi as Shika, and it bothered her. Apart from not knowing what was to happen to Shika, it was clear that Adjovi's mental instability had been taken advantage of and she was being set up to receive Shika's punishment. The transport cage was soon brought and Kabukor felt her mouth being forced open. She offered very little resistance, as the contents of a container, the same as was given earlier to Shika, was poured down her throat. It was bitter and she almost spat it back out, but with the way her mouth was held open, the only way she could get some reprieve from the bitterness was to swallow it quickly. From then on, she experienced a calmness that saw her drift slowly into what seemed like a deep sleep. The last thing she felt as she gave up her senses was her body being lifted and thrown in the portable cage. She knew she was in bigger trouble than she had been before, and from all indications it wasn't going to end well.

Vorsah was still furious for allowing himself to be caught in something he should have easily detected. He had allowed the fatigue of the journey and his desire for a hiatus from the burning sun to cloud his senses and let down his guard. He had just finished the arduous task of dismantling the hut, but it was all in vain as it served no purpose. Not that he expected that the situation would revert once he did that. It was more out of ire than anything else. Tired and extremely thirsty, he settled on the ground beside where he'd laid the baby, and signaled Avaga to bring him water.

"Here, take," Avaga said, offering him water from his pouch.

"You didn't fill any of our pouches with that water, did you?" Vorsah enquired with a look of sternness that Avaga hadn't quite seen up until that point. He shook his head, feeling too ashamed to respond verbally. He took a gulp himself, intending to wash down whatever remained of the water he'd consumed in the hut. He felt abused and uncomfortable in his stomach but felt even worse for placing them in their current predicament. His eyes drifted towards the baby, reminding him of its sudden, inexplicable growth. It didn't seem like a baby anymore. He was more like a toddler, only still succumbed to the comfort of the basket that held him. He thought for a second about asking Vorsah what he thought happened to the baby, but changed his mind realizing it would only bring blame to his door once again. After all, it all started after he drank of the water in the hut.

"What do you think happened to the baby?" Vorsah suddenly asked, as if to he could read Avaga's mind.

"I don't know but it seems he's grown even slightly more since the last time we noticed it in the hut." Forced to admit it, he added, "It's either he's reacting to this new environment or that's how he's meant to grow."

"Hmmm." Vorsah was already caught in a deep reflection of the whole thing. It didn't appear to Avaga that maybe they were in the future but he considered that possibility. In light of what he had just said about noticing more growth, he decided he was just going to wait to see if his growth rate kept up and then he would finally know if they were really in the future, or it was just the child experiencing growth spurts. Meanwhile they had to get ahead. They were clearly in uncharted territory with nothing recognizable in sight except for the constants of nature; trees, small animals that made occasional appearances, dirt which appeared sporadically, and a plethora of grass. Though the breeze was cool, the sun seemed to have held its gaze since they first stepped out into it, shining radiantly and without interruption. They continued in it, Vorsah, carrying the baby, and Avaga everything else. They kept on, hoping to catch the sight of a familiar landmark or at least of a settlement where they could enquire of their whereabouts, but nature just provided more of itself. After about three hours of walking and looking for some direction, they finally settled under some shade. The sun was still up as before and it was clear that the world in which they were was very different to theirs. They maintained very little conversation, as there was hardly anything to talk about except for the solution to the problem they faced, which they both knew nothing about. With nothing to say and nowhere to go, they both fell asleep under the comfort of the shade they were under, and so did the child.

It seemed like not a moment had passed before they woke up. The sun was still in the same place, hence their shaded spot was still intact. There seemed to be no track of time here but they arose, unsure if the rest was insufficient or if they had indeed slept thoroughly.

"Hello there," a voice suddenly boomed from behind them. If they thought they were awake before, they were now in a heightened state of consciousness. They were both up on their feet, turning to look in the direction from which the voice came.

"Did I startle you?" The bearer of the voice said in apologetic fashion. "I am really sorry, that was not my intention. Is this your child?" He asked, holding in his hands what seemed like a 3-year old child. "He was playing some distance from where you were sleeping."

Avaga and Vorsah were both stunned at what they were seeing. Here was a man who had just appeared from nowhere when they had spent most of the afternoon looking for some other form of human life. And what was more shocking was that the baby's basket was empty, an indication that the child the man held was indeed 'their' child. The sight of the child seemed incredible to them, as they stared long and hard at him, occasionally switching glances from him to the visitor.

"Who are you and where are you from?" Vorsah said, finally finding his voice.

"My name is Edo Tay, but everyone calls me Edo."

"Who is everyone?" Vorsah enquired further, with his look quickly changing from one of surprise to a more cognitive one, desiring to know.

"My family and friends, they're all back at the village."

"Which village, what is it called, and where are we now?" Vorsah seemed impatient with the man, and Avaga didn't see why, but he didn't interrupt, allowing their conversation to flow.

"You'll see if you come with me. It's called Abor. I know you're lost because it happens a lot here. I usually come here to help people find their way."

"You mention Abor but I've never heard of it. Which towns are nearby that are well known?" Vorsah, in every situation, was always suspicious. It was his nature.

Edo Tay proceeded to mention a lot of unfamiliar names, ending with the mention of Keta, the sound of which caught their attention. It all seemed too strange to Vorsah; the sudden appearance of the man in this place where the sun never set, suddenly offering them a way out. From his experience, he knew there had to be more to this than met the eye, but in that moment he had no reason to distrust the man. He sensed no evil vibe from him but, more importantly, he was their only way out of their predicament. Vorsah remained quiet for a while, analyzing the whole situation then he pulled Avaga aside to discuss a possibility with him.

"Remember when we were back at the shrine during the invocation when Hovinam promised to help us?"

Avaga simply nodded.

"What if the hut wasn't a trap but was meant to bring us closer to this point where this stranger helps us along. Maybe that's why I didn't sense any evil when I went in there."

Avaga simply smiled at this, and responded with a 'maybe' then started walking off in the direction of Edo, who was holding the child. Avaga reached for the child, and Edo Tay passed him over. Vorsah was visibly shocked with this move from Avaga and stood wide mouthed for a while. Avaga, who until that time had refused to even carry the basket containing the baby, was now holding the child. This was quite strange, especially after the child had experienced such aberrant growth; a growth which made Vorsah himself mildly skeptical of the child. He was shocked, but assumed it was because of what he had just told Avaga, that everything was being orchestrated by Hovinam to enable an easy passage to Keta. The child warmed up to Avaga, resting his head on his shoulders, an indication of comfort and trust. Avaga walked the short distance to get the basket.

"Let's be on our way, shall we," he said after picking the basket up. "We don't want to waste any more time than we already have."

"Yes please," Edo Tay agreed.

Avaga's decision to carry the baby and the basket meant Vorsah had to carry the other items. He carefully gathered everything and started out after Avaga who had already made progress in the direction Edo Tay was heading.

"So, how far do we have to go Edo Tay," Vorsah asked, after passing Avaga and catching up to him.

"It shouldn't be long. There's a secret passage not far from here that will take us directly to the outskirts of Abor. Once we are there, you're invited to either rest at my home for a while or just set off in the direction you wish to go, as I will show you."

"Good, so I'd like to know, what makes you come here every time, and how did you find this place?"

"Hmmm," Edo Tay started, "it's not so much how I found it but more who led me to it, because I believe the good spirits intended for me to find it for the sake of all the lost people trapped within it."

Avaga caught wind of the conversation and picked up his pace just in time to start listening in, as Edo Tay continued.

"Some months back, I traveled to a neighboring village and lost my way back. I had to deal with many nights of torturous weather, till one day I encountered a stranger who knew the area and how to get back on track. He guided me to a point close to a path that led me to my village, and I progressed from that point on my own. Close to my destination, but somewhat still far away, the skies opened, letting out rainfall I hadn't experienced on the nights I was lost, or ever before in my life. It fell hard and strong. I had to seek shelter immediately. It was in rushed pursuit of this shelter that I chanced upon the opening which is the exit I'm now leading you to. It's a world I never imagined possible, eternally sunny and it provided a great escape from the emotionalism of the outside world. I don't have to describe it, you're still in it. But of course, I realized later when I chanced upon travelers, just some random wanderers who couldn't find their way from here but were from villages that I knew, I felt I had to help them find their way. I had just been in similar circumstances and it's a terrible feeling. Hence my occasional visits to see who might need help. My visits here also provide temporary relief from the harshness of the world out there and it gives me a feeling of accomplishment and doing good which I don't get from anywhere else."

Edo Tay was as guileful as they came and completely sold the story to Vorsah who took it all in as truth. Avaga, who had also listened to the young man's tale, remained indifferent, more attentive to the child he had now mustered courage to bear in his arms. They travelled along a narrow path densely cordoned off by vegetation of all sorts. Avaga had to be careful not to bruise the child as the plants had their branches far out unto the path. They continued up to a point where the path ended in a mass of concentrated plant growth.

"Do we have to go through there?" Avaga asked, concerned for the child who seemed to be on the verge of sleep and would be awoken if they had to go through the seemingly impenetrable bush. The look on Vorsah's face indicated he held the same concern.

With a smile on his face, Edo Tay walked up to the edge of the bush and started picking apart what looked like carefully placed branches, revealing a rather narrow but clear path. Vorsah went first, followed closely by Avaga with the child, and then Edo Tay who placed the branches back in position as he also made his way through. The other side revealed a sight more familiar to Vorsah; a route he knew but hadn't seen in years. Not much had changed. Not much changed in these parts anyway, the most significant changes usually being the growth or disappearance of certain patches of the landscape's vegetation. As soon as Avaga came through, he placed the basket and the child on the ground. In the meantime, Edo Tay was also coming through and had his back turned to them as he placed the last branches to conceal the path. It was in that moment that Avaga picked up a large rock that lay nearby and directing it at the back of the squatted Edo Tay, hurled it with all the strength in him. Vorsah had his back turned to the action, as he enjoyed his familiarity with the environment. The noise of the impact and Edo Tay's sharp curtal scream brought his attention to what was unfolding. The sight was not pretty, as the sharpest part of the rock was what had hit Edo Tay, severing his spine. His blood gushed freely, soon making a canvass of his entire back and the ground around him.

"What? What did you do!" Vorsah shouted at him, a reactionary move more out of shock at Avaga's behavior than concern for the stranger.

"There's no time, I'll tell you along the way," he replied, as he stepped over Edo Tay's body and grabbed his arms and began to pull him back in the direction they had come. He covered the trail as he had seen him do it before he struck him. He then picked up the child and carried the basket as he had before, signaling Vorsah to lead the way and do it quickly. Whatever the reason, Vorsah assumed Avaga's action was warranted. He no longer had time to appreciate his reunion with the world he knew, as he led the way in the direction of Keta. As they both almost ran off, what they didn't know was that Edo Tay wasn't dead. He was bleeding profusely, as the stone had severed his spine. He lay on the ground within the bushes, his eyes were open and blinking rapidly. His breath was almost gone and he was quickly losing consciousness, but he was still alive.

While Edo Tay lay miles away losing consciousness, Kabukor was regaining hers, one she would have rather not come to. With her eyes growing accustomed to the darkness, she realized she was in a metallic cage, but chained to one corner of it restricting her movement. Just beyond her cage was another one and as she looked closely, she realized it contained another person. She couldn't decipher who it was, but she started adding things up and after a while realized it was the part of the palace she had seen the guards disappear into with Shika. She looked closely at the conscious but motionless body and she immediately realized that was the same pose Shika had assumed while they were back within the holding grounds. She amused herself briefly with the thought of how, only a day earlier, they had both been captives, but within the holding ground with others. She would have never imagined being here with her, only a day later in a separate secret prison, or what seemed more like a dungeon. Her thoughts were interrupted abruptly by strong sunlight streaking in, as the door opened and guards came through the entrance. With the guards bearing torches, the room was better lit and Kabukor could see more of what was around her. She noticed, with deepening gloom, that they were both suspended over, what looked like, a deep crevice, large enough for both cages to fall into. Her vision of its depth was limited, but she wasn't interested in finding out how far it went. She only wanted to get out at that moment.

"So Kabukor..." one of the guard's voices boomed through the room. It was Koku, the chief guard. It had been a while since he had surfaced anywhere. The last time being when he confronted Edo Tay at the holding grounds.

"Prisoners held at the holding grounds usually never get a chance of release. You get one, and you decide to come back prying?" He asked rhetorically, implying that Kabukor felt a sense of impunity which she shouldn't have.

"I was only looking to see if my brother had been captured, hence my release. What wrongdoing is there in that?" she responded boldly.

Koku was patient, after all he had the situation under control.

"You saw something you shouldn't have, and even if you hadn't, you now have, so it makes no difference. You should have just stayed at home under the protection of the guard assigned to you."

"So what are you going to do to me?" she asked, scared and teary eyed.

Koku ignored the question as guards all broke into laughter, a quick dry one. With that, he yanked at the chain that went through a lever embedded deep in the ceiling holding up the cage. It offset the cage, tossing her wildly within it; a source of great amusement for the guards who again broke out laughing. Shika was still mostly immobile from the effects of the substance that had been fed her, but she was slowly beginning to show signs of life. Her cage was still intact, unaffected by the movement of Kabukor's. Kabukor began to realize, in the moments her cage dangled dangerously over the crevice, how easy it would be for her to plunge down into it if the chain, held down by a metal peg, came undone. The door to her cage, which until that moment was closed, came flying open, but she didn't have to worry about falling out; she was still chained by hand to one corner of the cage and that held her captive. Her screams echoed throughout the small room but not beyond it. It was a very secure room, barred from any influences of the outside world. If she hoped for a rescue, it was near impossible unless orchestrated by one of the guards from within. Her cage was lowered by some mechanism and the door securely fastened before it was placed in its former position. Rattled, she lay on the floor of the cage crying. But the torment wasn't over. They tugged at Shika's cage, forcing her to sit up. Her back had been turned to the action, but she wasn't entirely oblivious to it. She knew what to expect and knew they intended for her to react in a manner that would provide them humor. But she was wrong; there wasn't to be any more humor. Whatever it was they were about to do, Kabukor's torment was just a comic precursor to it. They watched as the guards suddenly broke into a dance routine. There was no music except for the rhythm they created with their feet as they danced. The dance created the music and the music sustained the dance. Koku was at the head of the formation uttering indistinct words. His movements varied slightly from those of the others he was leading, but it was clear now to both Kabukor and Shika that this was a ritual of some sort. It wasn't terrifying to Shika. After all, she was a witch and had seen things she was sure these men couldn't even imagine. Kabukor's case was different. Her body shook in terror of what was going on. Beads of sweat had long formed on her forehead and areas above her breasts as she watched. As Koku continued to dance, he stretched forth both hands, then stood still. His body was beginning to shake, starting from his arms then quickly spreading to the rest of his body. His indistinct cantillation persisted. Then something happened that caught even Shika's eye; from nowhere a reptile-like creature resembling a small Python appeared in Koku's left hand and in his right hand appeared a knife. He immediately proceeded to behead the creature as he moved across the length of the crevice, spreading its blood, still engaged in his incantations. The creature was clearly under some enchantment as it wholly submitted to the will of Koku, offering no resistance and showing no sign of pain, as its head was completely severed, emptying the rest of its blood on the floor. With a blood curdling scream, Koku threw the knife and the bodily remains of the creature down into the crevice, and almost immediately signaled the rest of the guards as they quickly made their way out of the enclosure sealing the door behind them. Kabukor and Shika were too shocked to speak. They had just witnessed a ritual that only a priest should be able to perform, with the absence of a fetish priest in Keta for so many years, such ritualistic activity was supposed to be unknown to them. With their thoughts clouded with disbelief and uncertainty of what was to happen next, they just sat there, staring into the darkness left behind by the exit of the guards with their torches. Then it all started; the reason for the ritual. They first heard a loud slithery sound, an indication of an unusually large reptile. Then, as the creature got closer and the slithering sound became louder, an intense mocking laugh rang out, echoing and enhancing the crippling effects of the sound many times over. Even Shika was genuinely terrified. As their eyes grew accustomed to the darkness once again, the creature emerged from underneath the cages, revealing itself in its entirety. Not even Shika had encountered a sight like that in her lifetime. It appeared to be the upper section of a woman, but from her mid-section downwards, her lower body was limbless, scaly, and elongated. She floated freely in the air, her eyes burning through them with an intense stare. As horrific as she looked, she had the most ravishingly beautiful eyes they had ever seen. Her eyes glowed through the darkness, gorgeous enough to be a distraction from the rest of her grotesque body. After circling both suspended cages for a while, she finally stopped in front of Shika, producing a sibilant sound. In the next few moments, the door to Shika's cage came flying open and, as if held up by some invisible force, her body straightened up, stiff eventually leaning towards the unfastened gate of the cage. The look on her face suggested she was helpless and was up against a stronger force. She grimaced at the uncertainty of what was about to happen to her. With nothing between her and this horrendous creature, her mouth appeared to be forcibly opened, and her tongue pulled out in wait for what was to be her final experience alive, and possibly the most horrid. The creature moved close to Shika, stopping at the entrance of the cage as Shika's body was hurled in a forward motion by whatever force held her, stopping within an inch of the creature's face. Close enough to do what she wanted, the creature planted her lips firmly on Shika's and through suction, began to extract her innards. It was an evidently painful process as her body struggled to disengage but it was futile as, soon enough, she was just a literal body bag hanging from the lips of this abhorrent creature who seemed to enjoy the experience and seemed to have been made a tad stronger by it. What was left of Shika's body was let loose off the creature's lips as it drifted away down into the crevice below.

Far away, somewhere within the Eweland, Mamaga had already sensed the loss; the loss of her daughter and the loss of part of her powers, for they were inextricably linked. She had felt that part of her die, the part of her that came alive with the birth of her daughter, yet the power which she had given her never returned to her as it would have under the circumstances.

Back at the dungeon, the creature remained in the position, gloating and soaking in all the powers and evil that had come with her latest victim. Kabukor watched with great dread and trepidation of what was to happen to her. The thought of the death that lay before her was distressing, not allowing her spirit to rest. The creature then turned towards her and, with a smirk, headed in her direction. Kabukor knew this was the end and there was absolutely nothing she could do about it.

CHAPTER 10

Mamaga was throwing a tantrum, and no one could be in her presence without being abused; not even Kuvie who was new. She didn't know how to be sad, she only knew how to be angry. At the moment she was not sure what was happening, a feeling she had not experienced for a long time. She had no way of ever knowing what had happened in Keta, except she had sent Edo Tay there, and here he was in her secret chamber near death and being nursed back to health by Kuvie, because no one else could know about him. Earlier, after she had got wind of the encounter with Vorsah and his unknown friend, she had sent Kuvie to retrieve him; a task which was not unduly daunting because a medium existed through which they could get to him directly via the chamber. This was the same way he had first transported to his location. Her more-pressing worry at the time was Shika, whether she was actually dead or could the feeling be misplaced. A battle of indecision raged within her. If Vorsah and Avaga knew of Edo Tay and had dealt with him the way they did, she couldn't risk any more encounters with them, whether direct or indirect. She had to decide fast, and not even the ten spirits that resided within her knew the answer.

Meanwhile, the journey continued for the Keta-bound travelers. They hadn't had a chance to stop and rest, and neither had they broken the spellbound-like silence that had dominated their rushed journey since the incident. Vorsah had killed many times in the past, only ever for good reason, but never so violently. He didn't know what had prompted Avaga's action; until that moment he had seemed so innocuous. Now that they were in the real world, dusk was fast approaching and they had to find shelter for the night. There were many small villages along the way, but far off their path. Vorsah knew many of these, but until then, they hadn't stopped at any for respite or replenishment. Avaga also held his silence, waiting till they were properly settled to explain it all to Vorsah. He was just glad that the child had been asleep when he struck Edo Tay. It would have been such a traumatic thing for a child so young to see.

"Excuse me brothers, what brings you two to these parts? Are you travelers or just on your errands for the day?" a man asked from behind them. He had come from behind a tree they had just passed and was holding a crude implement in his hand that resembled a hoe. 'He is most likely a farmer,' Vorsah thought to himself, and felt annoyed that the man couldn't figure out that they were travelers, and wondered about the sudden inquisition.

As if he had read Vorsah's mind, the man went on, "I ask because, if you are travelers then there are no villages for many miles ahead and since the night is fast approaching, you might want to consider stopping at our village, which is the one after the next. Otherwise if you're from a nearby village and will be returning, then I'm sorry to have bothered you."

His explanation changed Vorsah's demeanor and also reminded him that people of the Eweland were generally hospitable, always looking out for each other.

"We are travelers," Avaga chipped in, "and we would be more than happy to spend the night in your village." He smiled as he said this, nodding his head at Vorsah to indicate his approval of the stranger's invitation. Clearly, Avaga knew something, and Vorsah was going to find out what it was. He proceeded to enquire more about the stranger's village, and after finding out all the details he needed, they set out towards the quiet, peaceful village from where the man hailed. It was completely dark when they arrived at the man's home. They were greeted by his wife who had an infant child with her, clearly their son. She had been worried, perturbed by the fact that he was later than usual. The conversations they had engaged in along the way was the reason and by the time they got to their destination, both Avaga and Vorsah already knew he had a wife and a newborn son. They also knew that he kept a small herd of goats alongside his cassava, pepper and tomato farm which he cultivated. His wife, like most of the wives in the village, would normally have expressed her full displeasure at the lateness of her husband, but the presence of visitors allayed that reaction. Instead, she showed a sweeter than usual side, as she offered them water and mats for them to sit on, which would later be their beds. The dinner she had cooked for her husband and herself was going to be hugely insufficient with the arrival of extra mouths but she didn't have to worry about cooking, as both Avaga and Vorsah were great cooks and mostly cooked their own meals. With ample foodstuff provided, they soon made themselves a feast. It was easy to decide what the child would eat as he was fed goat milk from the man's herd; something he enjoyed greatly for he slept soundly afterwards. As the night wore on and both children were put to bed, the grownups exchanged many tales of their adventures over the years. In all of this though, neither Vorsah nor Avaga revealed the reason for their journey, or anything remotely related. Earlier, they had both been offered wine, which they politely declined. They knew that wine made secrets float to the surface, and they didn't want to have to worry about that. Soon enough, even the couple had to retire to bed and Vorsah and Avaga were both finally left alone, within the small area created at the entrance of the hut for visitors. It was a small hut and under the circumstances, they had been offered very good conditions.

"You have something to tell me?" Vorsah whispered, looking piercingly at Avaga. He had waited for this moment all evening. He whispered because he didn't want to awaken the sleeping child who lay nearby. They had requested that their boy sleep in the same area as them. They couldn't afford to let him out of their sight and Avaga especially made sure he stayed within their sights.

"Just so you know, Vorsah, I had never killed anyone in my life until today."

This opening sentence just fizzled through Vorsah's ears, as he knew it was probably true, and just wanted to hear the real reason behind what happened.

"You remember that nap we took under the shade?"

Vorsah nodded his head in affirmation.

"Well I had a dream."

Vorsah knew immediately where this was headed, and he understood why Avaga had done it, but decided to let him finish, in case there was more to it than he imagined.

"In the dream, Hovinam appeared to me and she revealed to me everything that was to happen up till the point where the stranger met us on the road and offered us his home to spend the night."

Vorsah shook his head slowly in amazement.

"The man that I killed was sent with the intention to deceive and lure us. I know you didn't sense any evil in him but that was the reason why he was sent, so you wouldn't know. Hovinam's instructions were to kill this man once he led us out of that entrapment, or risk losing the child, and I did just that. I had no time to explain it to you as he was already upon us when we woke up."

Vorsah had wondered at various stages along the journey how Hovinam was helping them, as she had promised she would. He had initially thought that Edo Tay had been sent by her but clearly, he was wrong. They went on to talk about a lot of other things, detailing their plans for the following day when they resumed their journey. What they hadn't discussed, but knew almost instinctively, was that they would wake up in the wee hours of the morning and continue their journey while their hosts still slept. They knew by morning that the child would have grown even more and they couldn't risk anyone knowing about him. News about the extraordinary in these lands caught on like wild fires did during Harmattan, and the news of a child like that would spread even faster.

"Arrrrrrgh!" she screamed with all the voice she could muster, as the creature approached her. Kabukor had seen more than she could handle, and her thought processes were becoming addled. She had closed her eyes and the scream she let ring out from her lungs seemed to pierce the walls of the enclosure that held them. The booming laughter of the creature hovering above her effectively shut her up as she opened her eyes and slid to the floor of the cage, tears flowing freely from her eyes. She was defeated and hopeless and, at this point, longed for death to put an end to the mental torture she was going through. The creature approached the cage like she had Shika's, looking menacing. Kabukor just waited to hear that door open and whatever force it was that took over Shika to also take here over. But it never came. She didn't know how long she had her eyes closed but when she eventually opened them from her crouched position, it was Koku, the head guard who stood on the ground below her. The creature was gone. Confused and still unsettled, she looked around, scanning the entire perimeter of the enclosure to see if she was around.

"Stop looking!" Koku said with an authoritative voice. "She's gone."

Kabukor heard his words loud and clear, but she didn't care. She just went about doing what she was, looking around like a mad woman. The trauma was overwhelming. She eventually picked herself up and folded herself into one corner of the cage, looking vaguely into the air.

"You're such a lucky girl," his voice boomed through the silence of the hollowed space. "You escaped from the holding grounds, and now you escape being consumed by one of the most fearful beings alive." He capped that statement off with a laugh. Clearly, he was enjoying the control he had at that moment.

"I wonder if you'll ever get out of here, though." He was now tormenting her. "Maybe you might, but this time not alive, not after all that you've seen today."

If Kabukor was listening, she didn't show it. She maintained her unfocused look and involuntary sobs.

Koku had returned alone for some reason. The other guards waited outside as he came back in to check the aftermath of proceedings. Kabukor knew right from the onset of her detention in there that the Chief of the village, Torgbui Amada was not privy to what went on there. He probably didn't know that such a section of the palace existed, and to think that he'd lived there all his life, within the walls of that very palace.

"What shall I do with you Kabukor?" Koku asked rhetorically.

"Maybe I'll have your head delivered to me as my coronation gift," he said, and then paused, waiting for a reaction from her, but he got none, for she was deep in thought.

'His coronation?' she thought to herself. 'What was he planning to usurp the throne?' She tried to decipher what he meant by "my coronation gift" and thought about what she had witnessed within the past day. All she could come up with was the fact that the very happenings in that enclosure were a secret, especially from the chief. Apart from this, she didn't know exactly how he planned to use that in his favor. Clearly there was a great deal of sorcery involved, and the vile creature she had just seen was, in some way, shielded from the anti-evil machinations that had fortified Keta all these years. She raised her head and looked at him with a confused look on her face. That was all the indication he needed, and he began his explanation, proud and boastful.

"You see, evil is supposed to have its place in the world, just as good does. Evil creates a balance but unfortunately here in Keta, we have altered that balance with the creation of the holding grounds. Your own Chief Amada and those before him do not know the principles on which the foundation of Keta was built. It was built on that balance and that is what I will restore with what I have here. There are many things for which you are too young to comprehend fully, but what you saw today is a manifestation of what is to come." As he said this he turned to leave, apparently done, and that was when Kabukor spoke for the first time.

"But why don't you relish the prevailing peace and goodwill among the people? Do you want to destroy all that?" she asked emotionally, with tears flowing.

"You still don't understand, do you?" he retorted turning sharply, as if vexed.

"This is the opportunity for me to become chief; chief of a people who have lost their way and need to get back on the right path. Torgbui Amada doesn't know what he's doing, he's lost, just like the rest of you." He paused at this point and looked intensely at Kabukor, contemplating whether or not to go ahead.

"Many years ago, long before the priests of the Keta shrine came together and successfully created the holding grounds, the Chief's palace was the center of all power. In this very enclosure, as you witnessed today, they possessed their greatest asset, Amala, who wielded great powers. She defended Keta against her enemies and ruthlessly punished

anyone who dared come up against her. Everyone bowed to her greatness at the time, even the chief. But there came a time when the chief
died, and in his place arose another chief, his son, who wouldn't bow
to her greatness. This was the beginning of the creation of the council
to develop a strong antidote to all forces, hence the birth of the holding
grounds. When this happened, her powers were limited to a great extent
and the only place she found refuge was within these walls. She couldn't
go beyond Keta. The aura of the holding grounds was too strong for her
to attempt anything. So here she stayed, in this forgotten portion of the
palace, unable to do anything; until I came along of course. With the
promise of the throne, I have embarked to set her free by helping her
strengthen her powers, rebirthing herself in the process and instating
me as king. The witch you saw her feed on today, is just another in the
line of witches I've fed to her over the years as she continues to feed on
their power, becoming stronger in the process. I would have destroyed
the holding grounds long ago myself, but the magic in which it is embedded is ancient and cannot be physically suppressed or destroyed."

All the while he said this, he did so through his teeth with clenched
fists, a clear indication that he was passionate about this himself and
not under her influence.

"I will continue to feed her with witches captured by the holding
grounds till she is strong enough to come out and lay it all to waste.
Then I will be king with ultimate power over all the Eweland; with her
help, of course," he added, with a smirk breaking out on his face.

At this point, Kabukor couldn't be shocked any further by anything
after seeing the creature and what she had done to Shika. She looked
down at him with scorn, wishing him dead. He noticed the changed
look on her face and shook his head in disagreement.

"You shouldn't look at me like that Kabukor, you brought this upon
yourself; you and your inquisition."

"I was only looking for my brother!" she retorted strongly.

"I'm very sure he's dead," Koku said, "and I am certain you'll find
him soon when you join him on the other side," he said laughing even
more.

"He's not dead, he will come back!" Kabukor was not going to let him just say whatever he wanted but Koku knew he had the upper hand. He was the one in control.

"Well, the only reason you're not dead is because you don't have anything to offer Amala. She sensed that and spared you. You won't be so lucky with me when your time comes."

Kabukor wasn't afraid of the prospect of death anymore. She had encountered it closely too many times within the past day to be bothered by it. She decided to hold her peace this time and didn't respond to him. He turned to leave, closing the door behind him and shutting her out in the darkness once again. Immediately, she began to do what she had conceived. She started to gnaw away at the absurdly strong twine that had been used to bind her to the corner of the cage. It was a slow, painful process, and she bruised her gums many times over, but she was determined to free herself from the twines. A tremendous amount of pain, blood and saliva later, she tore free of the restriction within the cage and stood, deciding how to tackle the challenge of opening the cage door, which was also held by similar twines but bound together even stronger. She started stomping on the door to the cage, hoping the force of the strikes would eventually rip the twines apart. It didn't work. She settled on using her teeth once again; a torturous undertaking. The pain that accompanied the gnawing eventually became numbness as she tore through the tough palm twines, spitting blood and residue. After a while, she stood before the opening and looked down into the expanse that was below the suspended cage. Anyone in her position would have needed to figure out a way to get to solid ground after leaving the cage but her intent was different. She was trying to escape but not from this prison. She was trying to escape life; commit suicide.

Her last words as she jumped into the deep crevice below were, "I love you brother." Her jump was slightly off as she tumbled and hit her head hard on the edge of the crevice before settling deep within it. With a cracked skull and bloodied frame, she breathed her last, her final thoughts being of her brother.

CHAPTER 11

A week had passed since Edo Tay was sent on the failed mission. He still lay within the confines of the house of the Adzes, hidden from all the eyes except Mamaga and Kuvie who continued to provide him daily care. His back was healing but barely, and he remained on his belly, not only so his back could heal, he also couldn't move into any other position. He hadn't even managed to speak since being rescued. This very much irritated Mamaga who, more often than not, relied on the information that came from him. From all indications, the trio she had sent him after were still on their way. He hadn't been able to stop them. She had sent one of her birds, her many eyes through which she scanned and spied on areas all around her, and she had seen them still on their journey, unperturbed. This greatly troubled her, for the child was growing quickly and they were fast approaching their destination; a place where he couldn't be touched. She had not been able to tell her minions what her intentions were for the child. He was supposed to have already been there, feeding on blood; the blood that would adulterate his pure bloodline and effectively weaken him while they turned him to their side. Yet, no one dared ask her what had become of that venture. She had been in a bad mood all through the week and she had not tried to hide any of it. As it stood, they were already suffering the brunt of it. Only the previous day, one of her minions spent the entire day doing everyone else's chores because she had knocked on her door one too many times. Kuvie coped well even though he was new. He noticed her temperament and he dealt with her the way he dealt with his sister during times like this; he stayed away from her. He didn't speak to her unless he was spoken to. Although she didn't show it, Mamaga noticed Kuvie's discipline and respected him for it, however, that didn't earn him any special treatment, and Kuvie didn't notice or care. He had other issues on his mind; his sister. The period given him by Koku; the three market days had passed, and he feared the worst but he was still willing to give it a try. If only he knew she was already dead. He tried on countless occasions to get Mamaga to send him out there but to no avail. He felt useless, being unable to leave but constantly reminded himself that he would have been dead anyway if it wasn't for Mamaga. He had spent the last few days evaluating the situation within the house and how initially, the Adze's seemed so powerful, but now he couldn't do much about the current situation. Mamaga had no alliances to fall upon and they were left on their own. Kuvie was now already thinking about going out there on his own. Maybe if he could redeem the situation on his own, that would be his saving grace from Mamaga's wrath. If he failed, it would still be his death anyway. So, as he treated and nursed Edo Tay's wounds, he also plotted his escape from the camp. It was in the middle of nowhere, and apart from the potions that he had seen others drink that transported them back and forth, he didn't know how else to physically find his way from his current location. After careful thought and consideration, he decided going by foot wouldn't be the best option. Chances were he would end up in the same situation he was in when he was initially picked up by the Adzes. Mamaga was the only one who made and kept the potions that took them out of where they were. She guarded them closely and only made them while hidden away in her chamber. To get past her seemed impossible, and even if that was achievable, knowing which potions to take to which destination would be the next hurdle. He spent hours conflicted on what to do. The problem was Mamaga never left her chambers unguarded. There were eyes everywhere. Her eyes. He was sitting on a stool by Edo Tay when she came into the room.

⸺◦((◦))◦⸺

"Has he been able to talk yet?" she asked while scanning the room for anything unusual. It was an action she performed each time she entered a room. It didn't matter how many times or how recently she had been there, she would still scan the scope of the room to see if anything was different.

Kuvie shook his head to confirm her fears; Edo Tay was still unable to talk or move.

"I would send you out there but there won't be anyone to take care of him," she said.

For a moment, Kuvie wondered why she wouldn't take care of him herself. Maybe she considered herself beyond that. And he knew she couldn't assign anyone to take care of Edo Tay. After all, he was her secret, a secret Kuvie was privileged to know.

"But what if I could do what you wanted me to in a few hours, or even a day. I would be back before his wound dressing would need any changing."

Mamaga sat and thought about this for a while. She did not have too many options presently but everything aside, she knew sending Kuvie might be futile, as the evil that was now inherent in him could easily be sensed by Vorsah. As she continued to think deeper about it, memories of her daughter crept up in her thoughts, making her more inclined to making Kuvie go after the trio. She knew it was now too late to lure them to her camp, but there was still time enough for Kuvie to try to get the child to feed on the blood that would alter his intended path. In the end, she decided she was going to let him go after them but it had to be strategic.

———⟫《◉》⟪———

It had been many nights since Vorsah and Avaga had left their host family, sneaking away in the wee hours of the morning to save them from the sight of their abnormally-growing child. The boy, Amega, could walk now and had made a considerable part of the journey walking beside them. He had grown way too big for the basket, which was a good thing because neither Avaga nor Vorsah would have liked to have borne his weight as he was significantly heavier. He didn't talk but was able to make gestures to communicate with them appropriately. To them, he was a man in a child's body. He had already grown tired of the goat milk and now ate the solid foods that they ate, in similar quantities too. He had a voracious appetite, one that matched his growth rate. After the incident with Edo Tay, the journey had remained largely uneventful. Avaga hadn't had any direction or visitation in his dreams by Hovinam and neither had Vorsah. The days were ruled by long tedious walks along the dusty paths of the villages that lay along the way; the nights, by small fires, small jokes and short stories and insufficient sleep. They always had to move right at the onset of dawn to avoid any suspicion. The child, Amega, had grown accustomed to this and there were even a couple times that he would awaken them or be found awake when it was time to leave. It was only a few more days and such nights before they arrived at their destination. For Vorsah, it was going to be very emotional, as that was where he had made his home before he was forced to leave. He wasn't even sure how he was going to be received, but surely they would not even recognize him. It had been too long and the years had dealt too many lines and wrinkles to his face to be recognized. He was a far cry from the young Vorsah that left them many years ago.

———————

Meanwhile, back within the Adze camp, Mamaga had changed her mind about what she wanted to do. After careful consideration, she was going to do something that she had never done before; give Kuvie an antidote to the blood that bound him to the Adzes. She hadn't told Kuvie and wasn't going to. She just didn't want Vorsah to sense the evil within him. However, she also knew that once done, there was no guarantee that Kuvie would remain loyal to her and her cause. Vorsah swaying Kuvie would be as easy as the tall grass in the wind, yet it was a risk she was willing to take, for herself and for the sake of her daughter. She hoped the kindness she had shown him coupled with saving him from the icy hands of death would be enough to endear her to him all his life; just as she had done with Edo Tay, except that Edo Tay was only a child then, so she was able to mold him how she wanted. She disappeared into her chambers for a while, while Kuvie sat and waited by Edo Tay. He was still unsure what the plan was, but he would be more than happy to just get out of there and be on his way rather than sit helplessly within those walls. When she finally came out, it was with two small calabashes. She asked him to drink one after the other, specifically the dark colored one before the other which was paler. As he drank the first, he tried to determine what it was composed of by taste, but it was nothing like he had ever tasted and he could not identify it. The second drink, the pale one left him no time to think or wonder about its contents as it was extremely bitter. He was stunned by the taste initially but quickly recovered and held his face together. Even Mamaga had made a grimace in anticipation of him drinking it; she knew it would be bitter. As he waited for the contents to settle in his stomach, Mamaga briefed him on what he was to do.

"You don't have to worry about Vorsah knowing who you are or where you're from. Just pretend you're a traveler on your way to Keta. When you encounter him, be bold and don't act like you have any interest in him except for the mutual destination. I'll give you the blood that you'll administer. Be sure to put it in the food of the child when they are not watching. Immediately that is done, you'll drink this potion, which will bring you back here." She then handed him a very small gourd that was sealed. He was instructed not to open it till he was ready to drink it. It seemed like a good plan but Kuvie was disappointed that he had to return immediately after. What he wanted the most was to be able to go to Keta himself and try to rescue his sister, however, he knew better than to try to suggest anything outside of Mamaga's plans. He didn't want her changing her mind. Once outside, he could pursue his own agenda, especially after completing hers. He didn't have long to think about the situation, as he started to lose sense of himself. One of the two potions was intended to put him to sleep. Mamaga had packed all a man traveling would need and it would all be there by his side when he woke up, somewhere on the path to Keta. She looked at him as he lay slumbered across the stool, and smirked at the thought of what she had just started. There were several things she had not mentioned to Kuvie; the first was that he would lose both his identity and whatever power came with being an adze, all to avoid recognition by Vorsah. The second thing not mentioned was that the other concoction he had just drank was a trigger controlled by Mamaga; if he changed his mind it would be activated when he was close to the child. It was the last resort for Mamaga if the plan failed. Once triggered, it would kill Kuvie and whoever was in contact with him at the time. Mamaga had it all sorted out and she was smiling again. All Kuvie had to do was touch the child and they would both be killed.

⸺ ((◦)) ⸺

"I don't care if it's been a week! Send guards to nearby villages, find them both. What do you think this speaks of us as a people, that we don't care for our own?"

Koku nodded within his thoughts, but he dared not express it to the king. Torgbui Amada had been ranting at him for the past week over the sudden disappearance of Adjovi and Kabukor. Koku knew where Adjovi was but still organized a thorough search party for her knowing nobody would suspect her replacement with Shika. As for Kabukor, as he had gone in to see her, he noticed the open cage and the blood on the edge of the crevice. He immediately knew what had happened and where she had ended up. He was an actor and played his role well, faking concern for the disappearance of the two women. He even had two guards whipped; one for letting Adjovi off on her own after the incident which led to her mental debasement, and the other who was assigned to monitor Kabukor after her release. But today, Torgbui Amada, who had ordered the search for her after being informed of her disappearance, was livid that after a whole week, they still couldn't trace any of them. Koku's thoughts toward him in that moment were contemptuous, but he didn't let it show in his demeanor. He had respectfully lowered his head, as was expected of him and had both hands behind his back. After taking all of Torgbui Amada's chastisement, and being given a week's ultimatum to find both women, he left feigning a renewed vigor to find them. He knew he had to come up with something within that period to compensate for the disappointment that lay ahead for the chief. He went out into the courtyard, assembling all the guards except for those stationed at the holding grounds and those who never left the palace. He issued rigorous instructions dividing the guards into four groups, each to be headed in a different cardinal direction. He had to appear serious with his efforts at finding the missing women, and so far, his efforts seemed to deceive everyone. Most of the guards were in on the act, but having sworn a sacred oath of secrecy to die if they reneged meant that the secret was safe. He shouted instructions out loud to all the guard groups. They were to search as far as their feet could take them, for seven days before returning. He even promised a reward to the group that was successful in the search;

"The group that finds them will be honorably called out at the gathering of the people, and your pockets will be fattened." His guards listened unflinchingly knowing it was all a mirage. They gave away no emotion, all of them keeping a face as straight as possible. Koku himself was to wait at the palace and await news of their finding. He assigned two messengers to each guard group; lightning-fast runners who could deliver news to and from him and the guards at the castle. With everything set and the sun setting upon the horizon, each group set out, on a mission that most of them knew was futile even before it was conceived.

Adjovi had barely moved since she was thrown into the cage. Initially, her movement had been inhibited by the sedentary effects of the potion that was fed her, but the effects had long cleared. Her actions or inactions were entirely voluntary now. With her diminished reasoning abilities, she remained oblivious of the stench that constantly lingered within the holding ground and of her current circumstance or what had led to it. She was in Shika's clothes and her hair was disheveled, and looked nothing like her old self, as either a mentally deranged woman, or before, as a mother and wife. They even put the beads Shika had around her ankles on her. The semblance was cunning. For Koku, everything had worked out perfectly in replacing Shika so there would be no uproar about her disappearance. His initial plan was to fake an escape for her, and then use her as intended, which in any case would still have been a dampener on his qualities as leader of the guards and head of protection in the village. His only challenge now was to come up with a cover for the disappearance of the two women; relatively easy compared to explaining the escape of Shika, which would have also been a security concern. With the recent dispersion at the grounds and familiarity with the sight of the latest prisoner, the number of people who came to view the prisoners was steadily declining. Even family members of prisoners were giving up, as no one was ever released from the grounds. Kabukor's case had been different, and the circumstances that led to her release were devoid of family participation, not that she had any extended family to begin with; her only family being Kuvie. With this decline in numbers came a certain boredom for the prisoners, who became self-centered at that point, each focused on their own problems, and none paying attention to Adjovi. In the meantime, Koku had left the palace and was already home. His home consisted of ten unusually large huts, which were positioned around the periphery of the land it was on to form the compound. He and his wife occupied the largest hut with an extra one for himself when he needed to be alone. He had married his wife, Aseye when he was a young guard and they had lived in a single hut on the outskirts of Keta, but with his elevation came the added benefits, and over the years he came to acquire all what he had now. As with homes that had excess rooms in Adina, he had one reserved solely for his idols, sacred to his household and accessible only by him. It was there that he went to offer sacrifices and offerings, and prayed for success and longevity of life. You would think that with such an abundance of huts, he would give his two young daughters, Fafali and Zifa separate rooms to live in but no. He had them share one hut. The rest of the rooms lay idle with occasional occupation by guests or extended family members who were visiting. Koku was one of few men in the village who didn't keep a farm. As head of the Kings guard, he enjoyed many privileges similar but not identical to the Chiefs. And when it came to food, he never lacked it, as it was provided daily and in excess. His home also enjoyed the security of guards, but as most of them were out in search of the missing women, their numbers that evening were greatly diminished, with only a couple in sight. Koku had land to farm, but without the need to plough it, he rented it out to other villagers who paid the lease for it. The result being increased wealth which he didn't refrain from displaying. Most men who left home each day to go to their various laborious activities would leave instructions to their wives on what meal to prepare for dinner, based on what they yearned for, but Koku left no such instructions. He regarded his cravings as ever-changing and wanted every meal at his disposal for the choosing when he arrived at home and it had been as such for as long as anyone could remember. What was not eaten was given to the guards, and with only a couple on guard duty, they were sure to eat to their fill that evening. He arrived home to an array of dishes prepared by his wife and warm water ready for his bathing. As was his routine every evening, he went on to bathe, then came in and attended straight to his desired meal. His wife and daughters couldn't touch the food until he was seated and had served himself so they were always glad to see him come in, ready to eat. He didn't have time for small talk with his wife or daughters; at least not at the table. He washed his hands and was about to indulge his gustatory senses when one of the two guards on duty that evening rushed in. There was trouble at the grounds. There was a spectacle going on and it had attracted a large group of the villagers to the scene. The guard didn't have any details but anything happening at the holding grounds, especially at a time like this when their forces were diminished, required prompt attention. It wasn't only that, but also the fact that he had created a deception at the ground and didn't want that jeopardized or compromised in anyway. He didn't seem offended that his mealtime had been interrupted. There was a sense of urgency to his response in getting up and rushing to the grounds, which suggested to his wife and daughters he wasn't taking the situation lightly. They went as far as the entrance of the compound to watch him go with the guard who had come in to break the news. They all then returned to the table, with conversation and gossip as they continued to eat. When the women did it, it was often referred to as gossip but the men's were usually referred to differently; as meetings or discussions. Koku reached the grounds to find the largest gathering he had yet seen. It was even bigger than when Shika was first captured. He had already sent word for half of the guards stationed at the palace to meet him at the grounds to bolster those present there, who were barely keeping the situation under control. They met him there just as he arrived and led the way, parting the noisy crowd to make way to the spectacle that lay ahead. Apparently, Adjovi had regained her senses after more than week of captivity and was demanding to be let out, as she didn't know why she was being held. She said this amidst tears in remembrance of her misfortune with her husband and sons. She only remembered the things that happened till the point when she lost her sanity else Koku's deception would have been exposed in its entirety. As it was, people were confused, not knowing if it was the witch who had turned into her, or had mysteriously swapped places with the poor woman. They leaned more towards the second possibility because no magic was workable within the grounds. But it was also physically impossible to do so unless she received help from within, possibly a guard. So, many people in the crowd were coming up with many scenarios and reasons as to how it happened, but of course Koku knew exactly how it happened. He had a major problem on his hands now, a very unexpected one that demanded quick thinking on his feet. Soon enough, Adjovi was demanding to be taken before the chief. The crowd supported her demands, worsening the already ardent pressure. They seemed to believe now that it was really Adjovi and with her recent losses, the crowd, consisting mostly of those who witnessed it, were eager to get her out if it. Koku and the guards had no option. They were hugely outnumbered and they had to do the people's will. A message was quickly sent beforehand to the chief. There was to be a hearing and Koku knew that explanations and answers would be demanded. He had to come up with something.

<hr />

The journey so far had been long, but not as arduous as Avaga thought it would be. Except for the incident where they were trapped within the Evve, everything had been smooth. He wasn't petrified of Amega anymore and had grown to love him. He was a lot bigger now and would often attempt to talk, although the sounds he made were just mumbles and nonsensical. His gestures were easier to understand. It had been nearly ten days since they set had off from Adina, and they were only about three villages away from their destination. Vorsah was impressed with Avaga's attitude so far, although before they departed he had feared he would have had to deal with his needs as well. So far, he was impressed with his sense of maturity. The road they were traveling on was now very wide with sparse vegetation all around it. Mango trees dominated the scene, and had they not already had their fill of mangoes along the way, so they would have attempted to pluck some more. Starved of fruits and restricted to homemade dishes by their various hosts along the way, they may all have eaten too many mangoes, as their stomachs now began to rumble. They knew this would probably happen as they knew too many mangoes did that to the stomach. And pawpaws too, but they hadn't had any of those, else it would have been worse. The urge to egest fecal matter was strong yet one of them had to attend to Amega before themselves. Vorsah didn't have time to waste arguing who it should be. He picked Amega up and headed off the road in one direction, with Avaga headed in the other. After what seemed like an eternity, Avaga was the first to come back to the point in the road where they had departed from. When it came to matters of attending to nature, everyone tried to be as private as possible but it seemed Vorsah had gone too far out just to do so. 'Or maybe because he has to take care of Amega as well,' Avaga thought to himself. After waiting a short while again, he decided to go after them, and came upon them and the reason why they had kept so long.

"I could have sworn there was no one here when I first passed, but maybe I didn't notice in my rush to attend to natures call."

Vorsah, had come across a strange man who lay in the bushes, unconscious and bloodied. He was the reason for Vorsah's delayed return. The man looked beaten, albeit not badly, and he certainly wasn't dead. They could see his chest rise and fall ever so slightly in a breathing motion. Avaga made sure to take a good look around to see if there were other people in the vicinity, possibly those who inflicted the injury to this man. Convinced there were none, he came back and squatted by the stranger's side. Vorsah was quite the herbalist, aside from being the fetish priest of the village. It was something that went hand in hand if you were a great priest and he was. He had gathered a handful of herbs and weeds within the area, some of which he chewed and applied to the man's wounds. He then dubbed some manuka honey over this. Even Avaga knew the therapeutic effect of this type of honey and didn't know Vorsah had some of it. He wondered why he was surprised anyway; after all it was something people traditionally carried to deal with wounds or lesions of the skin.

"Why don't we give him some water?" Avaga asked.

"Not yet, he needs to awaken first, and aside from that we don't have enough water to waste," Vorsah replied.

This answer effectively ended any concerns about giving the stranger water while he still lay unconscious. It wasn't long before he started to move, more from the noises that they made than anything else. He had a glazed, confused look as regained consciousness. He didn't talk for a while, taking a rather long time to evaluate his environment before eventually asking where he was.

"What is your name, what happened to you?"

"I don't remember but where am I?" he asked.

"We just found you here. You're not too far away from Keta," Vorsah replied.

The mention of Keta seemed to jolt his memory.

"Aaah, that's where I'm headed, or was headed. I still don't know what happened to me. I live there; in Keta."

"I think you were attacked," Avaga chipped in. "Maybe from behind because you'd have remembered by now if there had been a confrontation."

The man nodded in agreement with Avaga. The man, was Kuvie. The confused look on his face was because he hadn't anticipated he would wake up and have contact with these two so soon. His understanding was that he would have to find them, but they found him. He was surprised about the blood and the bruises, but he reasoned this style of entry was something Mamaga must have thought of after he slipped into unconsciousness. He requested water. It was only then that everyone noticed he had his belongings scattered a short distance away. But this wasn't before Avaga gave Vorsah the "I told you he needed water" look. Avaga offered him water and they gathered his belongings, surprised they were still intact. Nothing seemed stolen. This hyped up Vorsah's curiosity.

"Why do you think you were attacked, nothing seems stolen," Vorsah asked.

Kuvie started to touch his pockets, clearly suggesting he was missing something; but it was all an act.

"It was my cowries, they're gone."

Cowries were the accepted form of payment for all trade, and to lose them meant that he had indeed lost something valuable. The various oracles and idols also demanded cowries more than anything else, hence its pronounced value. Vorsah had lots back at his shrine, all poured out before the oracle and no one dared touch it even though there was no supervision. The repercussions of such undertakings were often too severe and not worth it.

⟫ ⟪◉⟫ ⟪

"It was payment for this season's maize harvest that I went to sell over at the big market in Ada," the man said, referring to the village that came before the vast expanse of unoccupied land that they were now on.

"So, you are a farmer then?" Vorsah asked.

Kuvie nodded his head, the only truthful thing he had told them so far. They continued to console him as he continued his pretense. All the while Amega stood nearby, leaning against a tree observing through his small inexperienced eyes, understanding very little of what was going on. Kuvie pretended not to notice him. He didn't want them to even remotely think he had any sort of interest in the child. They finally helped him up as he asked them what their names were. For a while, they hesitated, unsure as to how to introduce the child. He lived in Keta and it was only a matter of time before he knew who the child was or was to be.

"We are returning the boy to his family in Keta," Vorsah quickly said. Any regular resident of Keta would have probed further but Kuvie remained disinterested, querying no further than he already had. With the blood washed off Kuvie's face, they headed back towards the road.

Vorsah and Avaga both hoped they could travel swiftly. The length of time left for the trip was short, and they hoped the new addition to their group wouldn't notice the growth of Amega, which occurred each night. They continued to converse, completely oblivious of the crow that had settled in one of the trees nearby; the eyes of Mamaga. It was to be that way from that point on; the crow nearby, stalking them and providing visuals for her. They soon merged with the road, in the direction of their destination. Kuvie was not nervous anymore, just unsure of what to expect. His assigned motive was different from his personal one, and that was still a conflict that raged within him. He knew though that Mamaga's watchful eyes were on him, and if this went well there was a good chance he could get his sister back. The incident with Edo Tay was still fresh on Vorsah's mind. He made Kuvie feel at ease, but deep within him he was still very cautious. He looked up to Avaga to see if he had had any revelations but he seemed very much at ease. Meanwhile, he engaged himself in conversation with Kuvie, hoping to discover any treachery, if there was any. It was in the middle of this that they noticed a multitude of people approaching in the distance. They were still too far away to see who they were, but that was the first time they had seen such a multitude on the road during the entire travel. As they got closer, the trio realized the approaching company was a group of guards, by their attire and their countenance. At the sight of this, Kuvie remembered his final moments in Keta and the pursuit that followed. He panicked, making Avaga and Vorsah think maybe that was the group that had attacked him. There had been no attack, but only Kuvie knew that. After verifying this with Kuvie, who confirmed he had never seen the approaching group, they walked on, Vorsah praying there would be no confrontation.

"Good day, my fellow men," Vorsah said as they got within a few steps of the group. Most of them burst out laughing. They considered themselves far superior to ordinary folk and mocked the fact that they had been referred to as "fellow men". After a few moments, one of them returned the greeting. The guards then proceeded to give a vivid description of the two women they were searching for. In that moment, Kuvie realized two things; these guards were from Keta and one of the women's description matched his sister perfectly. He wanted to ask more about the women in question but as he hadn't been recognized, he didn't want to risk being identified. After giving it some thought, he decided the person they had just described couldn't be his sister. He knew his sister would be held within the holding grounds, and it was a place that was nearly impossible to escape from. As docile as his sister was, he knew she wouldn't be the type to attempt it. Unless of course she was released for some reason and had decided to go looking for him. Avaga and Vorsah had already answered in the negative, turning to look at him for his response as well. He quickly shook his head indicating he hadn't seen the women either.

Meanwhile, Mamaga, with her bird as the medium, listened to all this. None of the descriptions matched her daughter. 'What if she had escaped, but was stuck somewhere, too weak to continue?' she thought to herself. She quickly shrugged the thought off, also sure that escape was impossible from the holding grounds, especially for a witch. She had not anticipated that Kuvie or his new friends would encounter guards from Keta. She also began to wonder how they hadn't recognized Kuvie if they were really from there. Maybe it was because his hair had grown a lot more giving him a slightly different look.

With nothing further to discuss, the two groups passed each other, each in continuation of their mission. Kuvie turned around one more time to look at them as they marched on but that was a grave mistake. He should have just kept looking and going ahead. The angle to which he had turned his head had drawn the attention of one of the guards, who raised the alarm and they were called back. Kuvie knew it would be futile to run. The road they were on continued for miles and there was just grassland in all directions. A series of questions followed, and with insufficient answers to disprove that he was indeed Kuvie the runaway murderer, they seized him along with his friends. Vorsah and Avaga were appalled at this turn of events, and tried to explain to the guards that they had just met Kuvie, but it was all in vain. The guards assumed that whoever they were, as long as they were friends of the runaway man, they were accomplices in some way. It was something they would confirm when they returned to their own village. Now, their original mission had to be put on hold as they had captured Kuvie. This was not the kind of entry into Keta that Vorsah had hoped for; in captivity. This was going to highly discredit whatever they had to say and he had to find a way to escape the situation before they arrived.

CHAPTER 12

Adjovi was back to her home, a free woman now, vindicated yet deeply saddened by her recent loss. It had been three days since she was had regained her sanity within the holding grounds and demanded audience with the chief. The process to ascertain if it was really her was short and simple. She was made to drink a concoction prepared by the chief's personal spiritual protectors, which would have been lethal had she been anyone else or had she any powers. The only confusion that remained was how she ended up there in place of the witch Shika. What was more worrying to everybody was Shika's whereabouts, and how this change had taken place. Luckily for Koku, Adjovi could not remember a thing from the moment before she lost her sanity till the time she regained it. The only other people who had the slightest hint of what could have happened were the prisoners at the grounds. Yet again luckily for Koku, they didn't care for anything except for their freedom and were oblivious of the true happenings of that day. In the end, the crowd was dispersed and Koku was called privately into the Kings chambers. Heaps of coal were piled on his head once again as he was given an ultimatum to find the witch. His entire being had just been shaken. From the moment that he was informed of the disturbance at the grounds till now, he had never been at ease. He went home, accompanied by a lone guard, the same one who had informed him of the disturbance. His wife had the table still set up for him and had reheated the meal but he had no appetite and went to bed that night on an empty stomach and a clouded mind.

It was often said that no matter how sane a former mad man became, there would always be a hint of rabidity that would rear its head from time to time. For this reason, despite the depleted number of guards, two were assigned on special orders of the chief, to guard and observe the hitherto unhinged woman. They guarded incognito, in the unlikely event that she was still Shika and had somehow found a way to outwit their evil-opposed system. She would be quiet for many long periods, possibly reflecting on recent happenings, and then burst out in sudden loud cries that traveled a great length of the village. This continued throughout the day. She was indeed a woman saddened greatly by her tragedy.

Not far across the village was Koku, still troubled and with a lot on his plate to deal with. In everyone's eyes, he still had Kabukor to find and Shika to recapture or offer a valid acceptable explanation for her disappearance. Despite all these, he had found another worry to add to his list; to kill Adjovi. He didn't want to risk her remembering the happenings during her period of lunacy; the exchange or the elaborate effort to disguise her as Shika. Already, she had surprised him with her recovery, and he didn't want another one. It would have been easier if the two assigned guards were part of his 'men' but these two were not. And they were assigned specially by the Chief himself. It was also particularly difficult because of the way they watched her house. It was difficult to know where they were at any moment. He spent many hours within the confines of his hut, unwilling to eat or even leave till he had devised a way. Eventually he left, but it was to attend to excretory matters. He still hadn't come up with a plan. He would have relied on Amala but she was powerless as long as the holding ground stood. This couldn't be done any way other than the physical. He was at a dead end and there was nothing he could do at that moment but hope that Adjovi never recovered her memory from that period.

Mamaga's plan had just suffered a huge setback. The guards in possession of Kuvie meant that he wasn't going to get the chance to administer the potion. What was even worse was that she couldn't rely on her last line of action. This would have just required him to be in contact with the child and she would instantly kill them both. Kuvie, who knew nothing of this, would certainly be glad that she didn't have that option now. She could still trigger it and kill him, but to what end? She only had till they crossed the border into Keta to do something; once inside, she would have no visuals or powers at all. The guards still had about a day and three quarters of travel before they arrived. Vorsah was also powerless as long as he couldn't mix up the concoctions he had in his bags. He needed them to make or cast any spells. At that moment, all their possessions were with the guards. They continued, with their hands tied behind their backs making it difficult for them to walk. The captives began to wonder if they would stop to at least try to look for a shelter for the night. But they knew these were guards; always looking to prove themselves in tough situations. They however needed to rest at some point. The darkness was soon going to be upon them and the darkness in these parts could be so dense that it was not even possible to see one's own hand close up. As the evening approached and the darkness began to set in, the guards began to realize their folly in not searching for a place earlier to spend the night. The winds that blew were terribly cold and greatly increased their desire to seek shelter. Soon, the rain added to their woes, further increasing their plight.

"I see a hut!" one of the guards suddenly shouted.

"Where?" almost everyone asked in unison.

He pointed to a bleak, far-off structure that could have been anything from a sand hill to a large rock. It seemed to be some distance away, but it was their only chance to find shelter from the rain. As they approached it, they realized it was indeed a hut. Vorsah and Avaga, however, realized something else; it was the same hut that had contained the water they had drunk and had trapped them within the Evve. Without saying anything, they looked at each other, both with the same things on their mind and the same look of surprise. Inside, the visibility was poor but having been in a similar position, they were able to easily make out the water jar that stood in the corner and the copra stacked closely together nearby. The guards all sat down with their backs to the wall while the prisoners stayed huddled together in the middle of the hut to stay warm. There was hardly any space to move around. Luckily, no rainwater trickled in as there were no leakages in the roof. At first the guards paid no attention to the copra or the water, but as the night wore on and the storm raged they decided that the hut had been sent from the gods to provide them with water and food. They drank of the water and crushed the copra, devouring all the innards. None of the prisoners, not even the young child, was offered any of what they ate, although Avaga and Vorsah would have declined were they offered. They knew exactly what would happen and in it, they saw a certain hope for their escape. Their only regret was that they would find themselves back within the Evve. It was indeed a long journey from the point where Avaga had struck Edo Tay to where they were now. And this would set them back many days. There was no time limit. It was only that the child grew ever so quickly and they wanted to be there in Keta before he attained full growth. It was important to show the people of Keta that indeed he was special. Soon, the guards started to fall asleep after deciding which of them would keep watch. The night went by quickly, and they all woke to bright sunlight streaming through the doors of the hut. Everyone, including the prisoners and the guards who had kept watch, had slept at some point. This was the first time in days that Vorsah and his group didn't have to worry about waking up at dawn. They were all rudely awoken by the guards to continue the journey. As they stepped out of the hut they were amazed at the view that greeted them. It was nothing like they had seen prior to entering the hut the previous night. Kuvie had been told of this place by Mamaga, but the hut and the different scenery didn't ring a bell to him at all. As confused as they were, the guards ascribed the changes they were seeing to negligence the previous night. They convinced themselves that in their rush to find shelter, coupled with the darkness and the resulting poor visibility, they had failed to notice the trees and general difference in the environment they had wandered into. They also failed to notice that the child Amega had aged a tad more through the night. Kuvie did, but pretended not to. After all, he knew all about him and part of his act was to show a total lack of interest in him prior to poisoning him. Vorsah knew exactly what was going to happen with the guards; they were going to wander on endlessly and eventually give up once they realized there was no way out. Hopefully once they realized it was some kind of magical place where the sun never went down, they would drop their guard and that would give them a chance to escape. So, the journey to find the road they were once on began. Mentally, Vorsah and Avaga were prepared for what was ahead so fatigue wasn't a problem for them. After what seemed an eternity, the guards started to argue among themselves about where they could possibly be. Clearly, none of them had the wits to recognize that they were caught in a trap. Another long period passed, by which time it should have been nightfall. The guards now realized the oddity of where they were. Having never before encountered this, they panicked, fearing that the recent capture of Shika was linked to their current situation. They began to tread with caution, making sure no further traps had been set up that could potentially kill them. They noticed that there were no other forms of life except for the flora, and were apprehensive of everything. They had taken their focus off their prisoners and had even untied the ropes that bound them. They soon stopped to eat. The guards had food; dried fish, *gari* as well as some dried fruit. They made sure the child ate sufficiently but as for the remaining trio, they gave them just enough to keep them alive. They weren't going to waste their food on prisoners, and had made up their minds that, at worst, they would cut them loose. After the meal, some of the guards, exhausted from the prolonged walk, slumbered off while others kept watch. Vorsah hoped that they would all sleep at some point. This would make it easier for them to slip away unnoticed and head for the exit that Edo Tay had shown them earlier. The guards, who hadn't even bothered to go through their bags had bundled them together with theirs. If the guards all slept, the trio would have to leave their bags behind. They couldn't risk waking the guards while trying to untie their possessions. Vorsah winked at Avaga and immediately proceeded to pretend to sleep. Avaga understood and followed suit, all in pretense. Kuvie, who had seen the indication from Vorsah reacted similarly. With all the prisoners 'asleep' and seemingly without a way out of where they were, the guards who kept watch eventually gave in to their need to sleeps. Vorsah had kept Amega close to him for this moment to try to escape but it was not to be. In the next few moments, they were all awoken by the noise of approaching footsteps and laughter. The guards were the first to jump to their feet. Avaga was slow to react, but Vorsah had already sensed the evil that was nearby. Kuvie also recognized the evil. It was Mamaga and a few of her minions. It was only then that he realized that this was the Evve she had talked about. Vorsah's charms and amulets were all in his bag and the guards' physical prowess was nothing against her supernatural forces. She had them trapped within her territory in a very convenient situation where Vorsah couldn't do anything. Everything had worked in her favor after all.

Three of the four guard groups that were sent out to look for the missing women were back in the village. As expected by Koku and those in on the act, they were unsuccessful. They were informed of the discovery of Adjovi within the grounds. Finding her had decreased the pressure that the Chief had initially placed on them to find both women. Koku still wanted Kabukor found, but he also now understood that it might be beyond the natural, especially considering the circumstances under which Adjovi was found. Koku, who had welcomed the guards as they came in, all at different times of the day, was surprised that the fourth group which had headed south, was yet to show up. He sent all the returning guards home that evening to catch up with their families while he waited in the palace square for the last group. After about midnight when they hadn't returned, he headed home. His thoughts were still very much on getting rid of Adjovi, but he still had his responsibilities to perform as head of the guards. He thought of Amala, hidden within the palace walls, but he had no business with her unless he had some more witches for her to consume. He had missed dinner for three consecutive nights, and his wife, Aseye, was increasingly worried. He arrived home to see her visibly concerned; he felt the same, but for a very different reason. Fafali and Zifa, his daughters had long retired to bed after having waited for him for a while alongside their mother. It was just the two of them awake in the compound, which wasn't uncommon as it was always like that before they engaged in their adult activities. Tonight, none of them was in that type of mood though, especially Koku. He had other things on his mind; things he had to do that very night that he needed an alibi for, in the unlikely event that he was seen. It seemed like an eternity while he waited patiently for his wife to fall asleep. When it finally happened, he quickly left, clad in clothes that merged perfectly with the night. He had been a guard for many years before becoming head and he knew none of these guards ever really kept watch past midnight. He tiptoed past the ones who guarded his compound into the night knowing that he'd return to find their positions unchanged. He was headed to Adjovi's compound. He knew from experience that even undercover guards sometimes slept at night. The ones who did were the worst at this offense. The night air was cold, like the intentions he had for the woman. He raced briskly but sure-footedly through it, making sure he would not be heard. More importantly, he made sure to cover his footprints. To make certain nothing could be traced back to him, he even wore footwear he had never worn before; to be discarded after his under-dealing. The house of Adjovi was fenced with coconut fronds, tight and freshly made, yet he found a convenient spot where he could slip through without upsetting the general structure. His heart was pumping hard and it sounded louder to him, in those moments, than his footsteps. He was a brave man but it had been many years since he had embarked on an agenda like this. Like many homes in Keta, the rooms had no doors, just thick raffia mats that covered the entrance. He had no light, as he couldn't risk carrying a lamp, and yet he had to find the room she lay in. It wasn't hard for him to do though. As he moved towards the house, he heard the faint sobbing of a woman; it was undoubtedly Adjovi. His initial reaction was panic. He didn't think she would be awake but it seemed she was very deeply aggrieved. He expected the house would be empty except for her and he wasn't disappointed.

"Who's there?" Adjovi shouted out in the middle of her sobs. She had sensed the presence of another being in her compound. The tone with which she asked the question made Koku panic. Unable to think or react to the situation quickly enough, he turned to go, but the woman was quicker. She was already at the door with her lamp. He had hoped he would be able to sneak up on her, but clearly that was out of the question now.

"Koku what are you doing here this late? Is everything alright?"

She had recognized him but this didn't cause her fear. On the contrary she was glad it was him. After all, he was head of the guards. Her only concern at that moment was that something had gone wrong requiring his presence. It was just such an unusual time, she thought. Koku was a very smart man and sensing the ease in her voice, knew she didn't suspect his intention.

'Everything is fine, Adjovi. It's just that with everything that has happened here lately, the Chief has instructed me to personally make sure you are safe. I hope I didn't startle you by coming around here this late."

"No, not at all," she replied. In that moment, she felt mildly flattered that the Chief would assign the head of the guards himself for her protection. As she looked at him, she thought it unusual the clothes he wore but she quickly brushed it aside assuming it was just his attire for the protectoral duties he performed at night.

"You should go to sleep Adjovi, I want you to before I leave."

Koku was a vile man, but having encountered her face to face made it impossible for him to carry out his plans. He would have to wait for another night. They exchanged farewells, each heading their own way. The night hadn't turned out for Koku the way he had hoped. He headed back, but not the same way he had come. This time he went through the proper entrance, but it now served as an exit. He had been correct about the guards who were asleep, but as he passed by, one of them woke up just in time to see him disappear into the darkness of the night. It sparked his curiosity and at that point he wanted to find out more. He woke the other guard and told him what he had just seen, and together they headed towards Adjovi's building to see what could have possibly transpired and if she was safe. As they approached, all they could hear was the sound of a woman in agonizing pain. Something was clearly wrong, so they decided to break protocol. They rushed into the dimly-lit room to the sight of a dying woman with a knife deeply embedded in her groin. They got there just in time to see her breathe her last. They looked at each other in shock but also fear for what lay in store for them for failing to perform their duties as assigned by the chief. She was dead and one of them had just seen Koku leaving the premises. The other questioned him just to reaffirm what he said earlier. He couldn't be surer. What they didn't know was that it was a suicide; the mental pressure of losing her husband and children right before her eyes had finally caught up with her. In their mind's eye, Koku had done it. Though they couldn't immediately see why he may have done it, there was one thing they were sure about; Koku had just murdered Adjovi. Nearby, just on the other side of the village, Koku had just returned to his bedding. He had gone past the guards who still slept and went to lie in the arms of his wife who was still sound asleep, oblivious to his night adventure. Koku thought about everything for a while, thinking about his failure to kill Adjovi, but he was a patient man. Eventually he also fell asleep, oblivious to what had transpired after he had left Adjovi's residence. If only he knew the storm that was to come in the morning.

About ten guards lay on the ground, all dead or dying. Nearby stood a laughing witch and her company but still standing was Vorsah and his group. The guards, unfamiliar to the sort of prowess Mamaga possessed, had succumbed easily to her will. Vorsah's experience in this type of situation was vast, hence the fact that they still stood. He was, after all, one of the main architects of the holding grounds in Keta. He had gathered everyone around him including Kuvie, each having a point of contact. The reason; Vorsah always wore a protective amulet around his waist. He only ever took it off to make extensions to accommodate his ever-widening waist line, or it would have been long buried in his flesh. It protected him from all evil and if he was in contact with anybody, that person too. And that was exactly what he was doing now. Mamaga had not anticipated that he would be protected, seeing as his charms and other amulets were in the bag; otherwise the guards wouldn't have been able to seize them in the first place. But killing the guards, though necessary, was the first mistake Mamaga made. Connected by hand, Vorsah quickly grabbed the bag which contained all his possessions. He rummaged through it quickly, and found what he was looking for; his band of feathers. It was with this that he could cast any spell he wanted. It was composed of the feathers of many birds, but predominantly domestic fowls soaked in human blood. At the mere sight of it, Mamaga and her minions started to retreat. Their loud laughter and gloating suddenly became silence, and trepidation showed on their faces as Vorsah started chanting. Mamaga knew she didn't stand a chance. It was for this reason she never thought about facing him head on in the first place. Vorsah's companions still held on to him, including Kuvie. He realized the balance of power had quickly shifted and he wasn't going to blow his cover now by playing out of character. But as Mamaga and her company retreated, she saw him as the weakness in the chain. She couldn't attack them from the outside because they were fortified by Vorsah's charm, but what if she could trigger what she had put within Kuvie. She could kill them all in an instant. And that is exactly what she tried. She had come out in the full glare of Vorsah, confident of putting them all away and she had to use every option available to her. In epileptic fashion, Kuvie started to shake, foaming at the mouth even before he fell. But he was the only one. The others were still unaffected because there was nothing within them. They were still protected from Mamaga's witchery. Vorsah, who had his back turned to the action the whole time, turned around to see what was happening. In that temporary moment of distraction, Mamaga and her crew fled, disappearing into nothingness. She had left them with the burden of Kuvie's death; a man whom they never really knew anyway, except that he was headed in the same direction as they were. For a while, everyone wondered what might have gone wrong. Kuvie was holding onto Vorsah just like everyone else, so why wasn't he protected? Eventually they let go of the thought as their focus went back to the child. They had been set back by many days and they had to get back on track as soon as possible. They found a convenient place to hide Kuvie's body. Though unburied, Vorsah went on to perform funeral rites for him to ease his passage into the spirit world. He performed similar rites for the dead guards, but didn't give them the privilege of hiding their bodies. There were too many of them to handle.

It wasn't hard for them to find the exit that Edo Tay had led them to earlier. As they approached the exit, they anticipated the terrible scent of a decaying corpse, but were surprised to find there was no body. Avaga, who had placed the body himself, was shocked and wondered if he had somehow lived and found the strength to move, or the body had been found and taken away. They didn't deliberate on this for long. They were happy to be out of that terrible place and back on the road. They had to be more careful now. The child was okay and he had seen a lot for his early age, but they also knew he was no ordinary child. Aside that, with the position he was being taken to occupy, there was a lot more to see than what he had had to deal with within the past day.

It was the morning after Koku had gone to Adjovi's house to kill her. Already, the news of her death was on everybody's lips. Of all the possible causes of death, suicide wasn't mentioned. For a woman who had just suffered the sight of the death of her family, and was recuperating from mental instability, that should have been suspected but the people of Keta loved controversy. They wanted there to be a killer even if there wasn't. The two guards who were assigned to look after her and who had discovered her body were already at Koku's house, waiting to inform him of being sighted the previous night, and how that implicated him. The plan was to arrest him and present him to the chief. He was head of the guards, but the death of someone at the hands of another in Keta was always punishable by death, no matter the culprit's status. Koku's late-night adventure ensured that he woke up late, but when he eventually did, it was to a huge gathering outside his walls as word had already gotten out of his possible involvement in the death of the woman. The presence of a crowd outside his walls surprised him but he was even more shocked to learn that Adjovi had been found dead, and even more stunned that he was being blamed for it. It was the guard's word against his and that of his wife and his personal guards. They all confirmed that he hadn't left the house after he arrived home. His personal guards also confirmed that there were no detours on his way home from the Chiefs palace the previous evening. Under the circumstances, it was easier to blame Koku's implication in the matter on wrongful sighting rather than his actual involvement. Eventually, the line of thought began to shift from Koku being guilty, to the assigned guards wanting to produce a culprit for their failure to watch over Adjovi and protect her. But in the village of Keta, once an accusation had been made, especially in the case of murder, a trial had to be held. It didn't matter if the evidence suggested strongly that the person was innocent. The case for trial was even stronger if there were no suspects other than the one accused. The crowd, considering the evidence of Koku's wife and statements from his guards, had developed an affinity and support for him, were following and chanting his name as he was led away. The tribunal had already been set up and the elders of Keta as well as its chief, Torgbui Amada had already taken their respective seats in anticipation of their rather unusual defendant. The turn of events couldn't be more sudden, as Koku's expectations for the morning were far from what he had foreseen. His expectations were that he would be within the palace forecourt welcoming the last group of guards who had been sent in search of the missing women. He was in the palace, but for the wrong reason; he was standing trial for the death of one of the women his guards had gone looking for. Usually, in cases of murder, a family member of the deceased would be the one to come forward to make the case against the accused, but Adjovi had no one remaining, at least not within Keta. So instead, the guards had to fill that role, as they had been responsible for her and had discovered her body. As Koku had not yet been found guilty, he was allowed to stand before the chief, in the middle of the gathering. He held his head back defiantly, not to the Chief but at the notion that he was guilty of the crime he was being tried for. The crowd support, considering the testimonies of his wife and personal guards, also gave him an air of assurance that the trial would be over soon and he would be free to walk out to reassume his role as head guard. At that moment, however, he was considered lesser than the average villager. So, the trial began with one of the two guards coming forward to make the case against Koku.

It was a simple, definitive statement; "I saw Koku leave the woman's residence and moments later we found her dead, stabbed in the groin." He stepped back after making this claim, affording the Chief the opportunity to pass any comments he might have. He didn't make any. He just signaled Koku to make his defense. As trials were a common thing in the village, every gesture of the chief during the process was well understood without a need for interpretation. Koku's personal guards, followed by his wife, came forward to reiterate what almost everybody there at the trial had been informed about; that he slept through the night and hadn't stepped a foot out since his arrival in his home the previous night. At this point, it seemed the story of his wife and guards were more credible, but the Chief also raised the question of why the guards assigned to protect Adjovi would mention Koku as the culprit. He was, after all, the most powerful man after the chief in Keta. Why did they not set up a more common man to blame. He called the other guard, who had also been assigned to Adjovi, to give his testimony, and that was when everything changed. The guard walked in holding a bag, and as he brought out what it held, Koku's face went from being smirky to a rather tense and visibly worried look. The sun was barely up, as it was still early morning and the air was cool, but in that moment, beads of sweat quickly began to form on Koku's forehead. He knew where this was headed. The guard held the sandals Koku had worn the previous night to Adjovi's compound. He had not thought it necessary to burn them, as he hadn't gone ahead with the plan to kill her, so he had worn them home. Unknown to him, the guards had picked up the sandals when they had been at his house.

"My chief," the guard began. "We retrieved these sandals from his home when we went there this morning, because we saw prints in the sand in his house similar to prints in Adjovi's house the previous evening. They size of the print and the shape of it were strikingly similar and we could not pass on it. Forgive me for taking his property without asking but it was necessary evidence in this case, my chief."

'In this case, it was better that he was asking for forgiveness, and hadn't asked for consent initially,' the Chief thought, and nodded his head as a sign of forgiveness. Koku from the onset of the second testimony from the guard had already agreed that indeed the slippers were his. It was something he just couldn't deny. But now it was up to the guards to prove to the gathering that indeed the prints in Adjovi's compound were made from those sandals. To do this, the Chief immediately assigned three of his most trusted elders to go with one of the guards to assess the print. The trial was temporarily suspended, as the quartet embarked to ascertain the legitimacy of the claims that had just been made. No one could leave except the four. They weren't expected to stay long. Keta was a big place but Adjovi's home was close to the Chiefs palace. In the meantime, Koku was offered a seat, something that rarely happened in trials in Keta. He was clearly jittery and everybody could sense that things were about to shift away from his favor. Soon, the guard and the three elders returned. The look on the guard's face was that of contentment. The look on the elders face, however, showed a certain sense of disappointment. A disappointment in the man they had entrusted with the security of the village. The trio resumed their sitting positions on the elevated seats, but not before walking up to the Chief and whispering to him what they had found out. The Chief still showed no emotion. He wasn't very old, but he was very wise and was not quick to jump to conclusions. He stood up one more time and recounted to the tribunal and witnesses what had just been told him. After this, he gave Koku one more chance to defend himself. The reason trials were held within such a short time of a crime being committed was that if indeed the suspected culprit was innocent, there was no reason to wait for the person to prepare a defense. The truth came naturally and without effort; it was only a lie that required forethought and careful planning. Koku at this point was at his wits end not knowing what to say or do. At this point it even seemed to the viewing audience that his wife and guard had lied in his favor. They had been truthful by what they knew but not by what happened, albeit Koku was innocent of the crime for which he was being accused. He began to stutter as he opened his mouth to talk, not sure of what he wanted to say. He eventually blubbered out an admission of having gone to Adjovi's compound. This drew a huge cry of surprise from the crowd, most shaking their heads at what they didn't think was a possible outcome. Koku insisted that he didn't kill her, that he had had a conversation with her to ascertain what had really happened with her but wasn't responsible for her death. There were unanswered questions that everyone wondered about. Why did he go there discreetly in the middle of the night? Why did he deny it so strongly from the onset? He was, after all, the chief guard and even if there was a pressing discussion he needed to have with Adjovi, he could have waited till morning to do so. In which case, he could have had her summoned as many times as he wished. His wife still stood close to him, but the guards who had earlier supported his claim had withdrawn into the audience. The chief, at this point, had no option but to declare

Koku, as guilty as all the evidence pointed in that direction. He was immediately sentenced to death, to be executed three nights later. Koku's daughters, Fafali and Zifa, who had missed most of the trial, arrived just in time to hear the pronouncement of death, and joined their mother who had begun to wail. Everybody watched in stunned silence as three other guards came forward and seized Koku. He didn't resist the attempts of the men. It was his wife and daughters who tried to prevent him from being taken away, but it took only a soldier to restrain them. Just outside the palace however, a large group of guards had gathered. A short distance from them lay several men, also guards. Dead. A mutiny had begun. The next few moments saw a plethora of guards rush into the tribunal just as the proceeding ended. The first to die were the guards who had seized Koku. They drove their spears through them as if they were foes, but these were men they had shared a lot of experiences with as friends and as guards. Next were the two who had brought the accusation against Koku. Before they could even gather their thoughts, a couple of machetes came down heavily on their heads, settling deep within their skulls. One of them died instantly. The other, however, continued to writhe in pain on the ground as his head was struck repeatedly with a machete. Those who had never before seen brain matter saw it that day. The Chief was still atop his high stool, stunned at what he was witnessing. For an instant when it all began, he thought it was an enemy attack but it was when Koku was spared that his eyes began to recognize the all too familiar attire of his own guards. He attempted to bolt but a sharp pain in his Achilles heel brought him to his knees. It was a spear. It had ripped the tendons and splintered the small bones in his foot. The pain coursed through his body like nothing he had ever felt before. He remained in the position he had been forced into for a while, screaming in pain till he eventually fell flat on his chest. He didn't see any of it but when he finally managed to turn his body around and sit up, all the elders were dead, murdered. The village crowd had disappeared and dead bodies had taken their place. Koku, who anticipated that this day would come, hadn't expected that his soldiers would intervene so soon. The man who had speared Torgbui Amada's leg so severely was now before him and just as he raised his machete above his head, he heard Koku's voice commanding him to stop. The guard was surprised at this command, as he knew that Koku wanted Torgbui Amada dead. He also knew that Chiefs usually had their own defensive voodoo to prevent them from being killed. It was usually either one that made them disappear into thin air in the face of danger, or one that made them impenetrable to any device of man's construction. In Torgbui Amada's case, it was already clear that neither applied. He was bleeding from a spear, and enough time has passed for him to disappear, if he really could. The guard kept his position as Koku walked closer to them. Torgbui felt that the end was near, but didn't beg for his life. He had seen too many things in his life to be shocked by a betrayal like this. He himself, in his early days, had enacted many acts of betrayal; a thought which nagged him in that moment. What had gone around, had finally come around. When Koku finally got up to where they were, he grabbed the machete from the guard and brought it down hard on the neck of Torgbui Amada. He had hoped the force of the single strike would be enough to decapitate the Chief but he had to wield the machete again to achieve it. He grabbed the decapitated head and headed towards the exit. He was looking for an audience, preferably the villagers but he found none of them. They had either bolted or been caught in the massacre. Those who had stayed at home had heard the horror from those who escaped and fled their homes. There was no audience, just him and his guards. He had hoped for this day and had hoped to capture it with the help of Amala whom he was slowly empowering till she was powerful enough to unleash her wrath and secure the throne for him, but it still felt good. Now he could do whatever he wanted. First on his mind was to destroy whatever power it was that fortified Keta, to release the beast that Amala was. Surely then she would be indebted to him eternally. But he still had to find the source of the power that had shielded Keta from evil forces all these years. It was a source that nobody knew about. The only surviving person in the whole world who knew all about it was Vorsah. Koku didn't know who Vorsah was and neither had he heard about him but he was headed that way.

CHAPTER 13

I t had been many days since Mamaga and her kowtowers had come up short against Vorsah and his companions. She was furious at herself for her failure. The ten spirits that lived within her had not been of any help and only stirred up inside her, urging her and telling her that together, they were powerful enough to go into Keta and take it down. Mamaga loved her daughter but she loved herself more. If only she knew her daughter was already dead, things would have been much different. Her minions bore the brunt of her anger in the meantime, this time more pronounced because they had witnessed her loss, a disgrace. She had also killed Kuvie. In vain. And there Edo Tay lay; immobile and paralyzed and was her burden alone to bear. She felt her options were exhausted but she wasn't going to give in that easy. She had spent many days in her chambers enraged, watching Edo Tay but paying him no attention. She watched him day and night as the fetor from his wounds grew worse. He was slowly dying and Mamaga watched, somehow drawing strength from the neglect and depravity she showed. When he died a few days after, that was her cue to go to Keta and rescue her daughter. She left him there to rot, her thought processes greatly influenced by desire and the ten spirits of her family that inhabited her. Her channels of travel, making distance inconsequential, was one of her fortes and she was going to go ahead of Kuvie and Vorsah, rescue her daughter and possibly devise a plan to wait in ambush for that approaching group. She made sure to drink all the potions that fortified her as well. Without farewell, she left the Adzes, on a mission to recover her daughter and her sense of pride.

Just outside of Keta a small group of men who had earlier fled their homes during the slaughter in the chief's palace in Keta were regrouping themselves in preparation to revisit the situation in Keta. These men were clearly distressed and had no weapons but they had numbers. Fast approaching was Vorsah, Avaga and the child, Amega, who had aged considerably, and was now a 15-year old boy. They had been more careful this time on the resumption of their journey and had slept mostly by the wayside, completely avoiding interaction or admission into any home. This aided their travel time significantly and brought forward their arrival time. It was only about half a day more and they would be in Keta. The way ahead was seemingly clear for the safe passage to Keta, but as the road made a turn they again noticed a group of men, who at the same time noticed them. Vorsah reacted first, immediately bringing out his band of feathers. This time he was ready to cast a spell on anyone in order to make progress with their entry into Keta. With memories fresh on their minds of what had happened with the guards, they weren't taking any chances. The sight of two men and a young boy approaching was hardly a distraction for these men, who were more focused on their problems back home. As the trio approached, the men paid them no heed, and continued their animated discussion on what had just happened back home and how to reclaim their village from oppression and forced rule. Vorsah, listened to the rather loud rumblings of the crowd and realized that these men posed no threat to them, so he lowered his band of feathers, which still held in case he was required to immediately use it. There was clearly some sort of agitation going on and they listened in. They soon got the hang of it; Keta was under siege by the same people trusted to protect it. This threatened to lay waste to the purpose of their trip, as they knew they couldn't venture into Keta under these circumstances. They would be mistaken for tricksters or spies, which was anything but their real intentions. Vorsah and Avaga exchanged glances, both looking confused at the thought of what lay ahead. From what they gathered, this had happened a day earlier and they both shuddered at the thought of what would have happened had they not been delayed by the guards and gotten to Keta a few days earlier. They probably would have been caught in the middle of all the brouhaha and could have been killed. Or maybe they would have been their saviors of the situation. Vorsah played with all these scenarios in his head while he thought of a way around their current predicament. Having finally gathered his thoughts, he spoke out boldly to the hearing of the crowd.

"People of Keta, I greet you."

Everyone turned around instantly to catch a glimpse of this bold, new voice.

"I am myself a son of Keta, but long departed from the village and only returning now. It is sad to hear of your misfortune, but I believe we were sent opportunely to help you out of this situation." As he spoke, there was a deafening silence, even as he had paused. Then as if orchestrated, they all broke out into delirious laughter. Their situation was dire and precarious, but the sight of a wiry old man, accompanied by a sheepish looking young man and a boy promising them redemption was just too amusing. This irritated Vorsah, who had very little patience for mockery. It took every nerve in his body to refrain from using his band of feathers to quieten the crowd and show them what he was capable of.

"Move along old man," one man in the crowd, apparently, the leader said. "We have no time for small talk or for entertainment."

"You think I am joking?" Vorsah shouted angrily. He hated to be taken lightly. This time, he was going to use his feathers. He lifted it high above his shoulders, but before he could utter any words at all, a female voice caught everyone's attention.

"Listen to him, you fools! Listen before the hand of extinction falls heavily on every one of you. You have been warned and it will only be this one-time."

The voice had come from behind them and they turned just in time to see a dissipating apparitional figure high above their heads. The trio, who were facing the crowd had seen it all, and they saw who it was; Hovinam. She was contributing her quota as promised. Everyone in the crowd was stunned particularly because there were no women in their midst. They had all been left in a secret cove some distance from where they were on the road. After a little while, they began to mumble among themselves, wary of the possible prowess of this old man who they had until that moment, seen as ordinary.

"Who are you?" one of the men asked from within the gathering. They had a look that was a mixture of fear and hope but more inclined to the former.

"I am Vorsah, this is Avaga and the child you see is Amega. He is the reason why we embarked on this trip in the first place." He went on to reveal the purpose of the child and had Avaga narrate to them, the circumstances surrounding his acquaintance with the child.

"As we travel down this road together overnight, you will know by morning why this child is a special one." He was referring to Amega's expected growth spurt which usually happened overnight. For the moment, that was all that really marked him as a special child, his remarkable growth rate. For the men within the crowd, Keta had never needed a priest for its shrine, nor had they witnessed the presence of one there all their lives. All their spiritual problems had been taken care of by the existence of the holding ground. But things were changing and with the recent takeover, they feared the holding ground would be destroyed as well. They began to see the sense and timeliness of the arrival of the trio. A few speeches later, Vorsah was made the leader of the group.

"Bring them out, all of them!"

Koku was angry. He was preparing to have all the prisoners within the holding ground killed. All the prisoners who remained had no special powers, neither were they being held because that. They were serving various sentences for domestic offenses.

"Hang them all and pile their bodies atop the others. We have no need for them. They drain our resources."

Koku had started his reign with a viciousness that had never been seen. He was no longer a man and no different from a savage. His wife and daughters in that moment were at home, guarded yet terrified of the man who they knew as husband and father. They all looked at each other, their eyes glossy from the tears they had cried all morning. They each knew they would be miles away from where they sat were it not for the guards; running and scared but probably no more scared than they already were. The holding grounds could easily have been renamed the killing grounds on this day, as the guards carried out their orders. Body after body slumped to the ground, cut loose from the ropes that had yanked the lives out of them. No mercy was shown, as even the old among them were treated harshly; manhandled and treated in the same manner as all the others. The oldest ones were the ones they feared most since they were more easily tagged as witches and wizards. As the day wore on, the bodies piled up. There were no mourners and no audience, just the perpetrators. And the dead. After the last body had been added to the mountain of humans, they sought to burn the entire pile, together with the holding ground in the hope that the desecration of it would suck its power and render it useless.

"Get the tar," one of the guards shouted. "And flaming torches."

Koku had already designated one of the other guards to act on his behalf. This wasn't necessarily in case he was absent, but was intended to create a situation where he couldn't be spoken to directly except through the designated guard. He was preparing himself for kingship but even the other guards knew that he wanted more; he wanted to be a god.

Just beyond the holding grounds, a pair of eyes peered through the woods assessing all that was happening, and contemplated what measure to undertake. The sight of men and women dying and the morbidity that lingered in the air was exactly what her spirit thrived on. Mamaga had dared to breach the boundaries of Keta and she was on the verge of entering the most feared territory for her kind. Koku and the guards, oblivious to any observers, continued their rancor. The tar had been brought and the torrid smell of human flesh had encapsulated the grounds already and was gradually inundating the rest of the village. At this moment, Mamaga made her move, taking bold but cautious steps towards the grounds. As baneful as she was, it was a mother's love for her child that drove her on. The sight of her clearly spelt witch, but with the searing heat that had engulfed the entire ground, no one dared get close to her. Spears tore through the blaze, in search of her matter but found none. Mamaga was amazed at the power which she felt. Clearly, she was using her own powers to protect herself from the flesh-fueled flames that ravaged everything around her, but to feel a surge in power, especially in a place that had weakened all her kind before her, was something she never fathomed. Koku looked at her in amazement. He couldn't believe what he was witnessing. Through the heat shimmer they both locked eyes; Koku and Mamaga, one bound by a new-found fear and the other a resurgent dominance. Koku's apperception of the situation was that his desecration of the holy grounds with dead bodies and subsequent torching was the reason the witch now walked freely within the holding grounds. For Mamaga, she sensed, for the first time in a long time, the forces of the spirits within her coming together to defy the usually overwhelming power that had for so many years apprehended those before her. She was, after all, inhabited by ten spirits, her own not included. Panic, coursed through the bloodstream of the guards as freely as the billowing smoke that was quickly filling up the airspace around the grounds and beyond. And just like the smoke, the guards found random direction, each running where the wind took them, confused and unsettled. Koku however, stood his ground. After all this was his mission, his home and all witches he had encountered before today had bowed to him. He was sure he would find his way with this one too. So far, Mamaga had been pleasantly surprised but she didn't show it. She had noticed the dispersion of the soldiers and the fear that accompanied their actions. She had also noticed the presence of the one man who remained; Koku. She moved towards him. She only sought answers at this point; answers that would help her find her daughter. Koku waited till she was just a few steps from him and then ever so calmly, turned around and started walking away. He was heading for the hidden spot behind the Kings palace that held Amala. It was a long walk, far too long for him to make it there without being stopped by Mamaga. To him, if the effects of the holding grounds had been nulled and Mamaga, walked freely, so could Amala. Mamaga already had her sights on him, following closely and despite her apparent advantage she approached the situation with a heightened sense of caution. It was all too easy for her to believe it entirely. She allowed Koku to walk, but he dared not turn around to look lest the trepidation in his eyes be exposed. The action in itself was sure to reveal a frailty in the show that he was putting on. His eyes were dead-set on the path leading to the secret cove underneath the palace, with Mamaga's eyes on him. With slow uneasy

attention the most while he loitered on the outskirts awaiting his turn to make his entry.

The king's guard and messengers meanwhile, also having travelled far and wide in pursuit of them, finally returned home with the disappointing news of their inability to find them. The king, while glad that Ama would no longer be in his sight, feared the possibility of what Vorsah knew and what he could be up to. This was a great source of worry to him.

It had been a whole moon since Vorsah had let Ama and the twins enter the village ahead of him. He didn't want the connection drawn at all and knew that the sight of a lone woman with two infants would surely draw sympathy and help. He sneaked into the village at night sometimes in hopes of finding out about their current state, but it was difficult to do without intruding obstructively, therefore he kept his distance.

As he reentered the village again, this time in broad daylight, he was sure it wouldn't be long before he saw them once again.

As was custom with most places around that time, visitors were always welcomed and treated with utmost respect, unless they gave their hosts a reason not to, in which case it could all turn around quickly. Visitors were always traditionally taken to the chief's palace, not necessarily to see the chief but the chief's palaces usually had quarters for strangers. It was usually the best place to have a stranger reside, as it was the most protected area of the village. Vorsah was taken to one such portion of the palace where he could clean himself up, and food was provided to sate his hunger. It was also the custom to make sure a stranger was well catered to and comfortable before any queries were made of his visit. While he did all this, Vorsah kept his eyes and ears open for any indication of the mother and her twins, but there was none. If he was right, she would still be residing in the chief's quarters as well, unless someone within the community had volunteered to host her or she had already been provided a home of her own. The thought of that was not far-fetched as it had been a month already since she had entered the village. By now, Vorsah had concocted the perfect story to tell the villagers as to why he was there. He was, after all, planning to stay for good. Everything he told them was truthful. He informed them he was a priest, and with his band of feathers, there was very little he could not do to prove it. He performed a few wonders with his band of feathers to that effect. He knew this place did not have a priest of its own. He sensed it as he came in. Had there been one, he would not have shown disrespect by presenting himself as another. Priests had very low tolerance for other priests who invaded their territory, and being one, he knew it well enough. He claimed he had been sent from a very far off place by the gods, to protect someone who was also being sent to them. This far-off place he so vaguely described to them that they did not care to give much thought to find out where it really was. He had, after all, proven that he was a tool of the gods, and at this point they doubted nothing of what he told them. It was when he told them who he was sent to protect that he got the biggest surprise of his life.

Ama was dead. She had been murdered along with one of her twins. The only reason the other child survived was because he was mistaken for dead, but had been severely wounded, as he had been stabbed in the thigh. He was now under the care and protection of the chief's very own nurses. It was unheard of that such a thing happened to strangers, but this had happened under their very noses while the mother had stepped outside of the confines of the palace, for what reason they were still unsure about. They had tried in the days after her death to solve the mystery but nobody knew anything about it. Some of the villagers did not even know she was there and was being accommodated at the chief's palace prior to her death.

"Avaga, you were that surviving twin." Amega told the whole group. At this point, Vorsah's tears streamed down his face, and Avaga just stood in shock and disbelief at what he had just heard.

"After this, Vorsah stayed and swore to find the killer, but he was never able to. He suspected it could have been Amada but he knew they had traveled too far for him to have been guilty of it. I am your twin Avaga and mom and I have looked over you all these years, and Vorsah too. It was time we brought you to your truth. You are the rightful heir to the throne in this kingdom."

All the men in the room were in shock; everybody except Amega.

He was not a man, he was a spirit, the ghost of the murdered twin. Avaga now understood why he was always the floating child, moving from home to home. He also now understood why, despite no parental guidance, he never suffered being a floater. He was being looked after. He now knew who his parents were. His father had been king. He was a prince.

"Everything that has happened so far was intended to lead us to this moment right here."

As Amega said this, he completely dismantled the entrance to their cage hurtling about three guards with it, all with the wave of his hand. He held a power even Vorsah couldn't compete with. It didn't make sense what they were being held for and why they had to be held. The sudden activity froze the guards to the spot as the men marched out bolstered by the new-found energy from Amega's story. It wasn't only the activity; Amega had a part to play as the men seized all the guard's weaponry. These people were not enemies. They were supposed to be brothers and family members but they had been corrupted. It seemed like they had a certain shade cast over their eyes. As they were all rounded up by the men, it seemed to clear up as they all stood, dumbfounded and looking around them, trying to make sense of what was happening. The holding grounds had been forever desecrated, rid of its powers and it was no more a place that rid people of their power. The men chanted with joy as it seemed everything was returning to normal. At the same time, the women and children who were in the bush were returning to the village, unknowingly led on by the spirit of the ghost mother who was bringing them back safely to the comfort of their village. By this time, Avaga had been hoisted on the shoulders of some of the men as they chanted and praised him as king. Vorsah looked on and, as he took his eyes off Avaga and tried to look for Amega, he realized he was gone, nowhere in sight. He heard what he thought was his name and as he turned around, he barely saw the disappearing image of the ghost mother, walking off in the distance. Her job had been done. She had returned her son to his rightful place and had nothing more to hold unto this world. Amega wasn't gone as Vorsah had thought. As a spirit and according to an age old prophesy, he was to head the shrine in Keta and to protect his brother's rule. To do this, he had inhabited Vorsah's body. Vorsah felt the power and they were one now. No one else would know this except him.

Three moons had passed since Avaga had been made king. Vorsah, inhabited by Amega, had resumed his position as chief priest of the land of Keta, and once again all was well on the land. The people were happy. The area that was the holding grounds became now a memorial ground for all lives that had been lost there. Even though Vorsah knew the old secrets of the magic that had created a place like the holding grounds, he had no reason to. He was back in charge at the shrine and would take care of what needed to be. However, he made a few changes for the protection of the village. For the first time, he trained other sub priests who wielded power similar to his. In the event of an attack or invasion, combined, they wielded enough power to bring any person or spirit down. It was unprecedented for priests to do this, but this was a new era and he knew enough from having been around so long to know what would work. Avaga also made a lot of new changes for the betterment of the village, but the most significant; he had his name changed. He was no longer to be called Avaga, which meant big penis. He never found out why he had come to be called that. His name from now on would be Dzidulah, which meant Victor!

THE END